Primordial Fall

Gwydion Royce

ORACLE OF LOST PATHS BOOKS

Cover Design by Damonza.com

1st edition 2024

Oracle of Lost Paths Books

author@gwydionroyce.com

979-8-9916145-4-2 (eBook)

979-8-9916145-5-9 (Paperback)

CHAPTER ONE

Meg

I balked. "What?" Yes, I'd been warned about Hades's unusual change of mindset, but still...

"We've been around for far too long. It's time to pass the torch. This endless existence drags. It's torture. Every day, the same, except for whatever drama we can rustle up." He scoffed. "It's no wonder people are increasingly angered at us all the time."

"Do *all* of you feel the same?"

"I can't speak for everyone. But quite a few."

I hesitated.

"Please, speak your peace," he offered.

"I mean, if you really wanted out..."

A grin twisted his face, almost rueful. "Spoken like someone with a fundamental misunderstanding of the gods."

I crossed my arms. "Enlighten me."

"What I'm talking about is not true death. If a god kills a god, then it's game over. It's oblivion. We cease to exist on every level." He leaned forward, a manic gleam in his eye. "What I'm asking for is resurrection. A restart. We get to join the other souls as they make their journeys. Born again to live, and die, and live again. Always something new."

I released a steady breath. "How closely do you pay attention to mortal lives?" I spoke carefully. No need to push unnecessary buttons.

"What does that matter?" he asked.

"Because I would bet that most people wouldn't see the constant repetition of the pain and suffering of everyday life as a gift. But then again, you always want what you can't have. You see mortality as a gift, the same way *they* see immortality."

"But it all leads to a reward, does it not? Even the most menial, seemingly worthless lives matter in the end. The resurrection machine spits them out into eternity. Nameless, shapeless. Rejoining with that singular consciousness and knowing only bliss. Never again tied to anything physical."

Of all the things I imagined I'd be doing, having a deeply philosophical discussion with Hades in a tea room was not on that list.

"Why do you think the Titans can do this for you?"

"They are the most powerful beings remaining. If they can't, nobody can."

"You're the Lord of the Dark. The underworld is your domain. That's a pretty humbling thing for you to say."

"Or insane." He leaned back. "That's what you really want to say, isn't it?" He gave me a lazy smile, swirling his fingers around the pattern on the sofa.

"I'm just trying to figure you out. It's certainly something we can discuss further. Once the Titans are freed."

"Of course. Do I have your word on that?" he asked.

I nodded. "That I'll try? Yes."

"Excellent! That's all I ask," said Hades, spreading his arms wide.

"So am I free to go?" I asked, hopeful. I'd been surreptitiously trying to access the stream of time since the creepy construct shut down my portal, but so far no luck. It wouldn't be hard for someone as powerful as Hades to shut down all travel in and out by way of gates and portals if he so chose. It was already harder than average, had to be, otherwise all the souls in here would just walk right out again.

"Not yet. You need to stay awhile. So I can get a better gauge of your character."

"And if you don't like what you find?" I watched him curiously. "It'll be hard for me to free the Titans from here."

He waved me off and got to his feet. "We'll worry about that later. Now come. Let's take a tour, shall we?"

I followed him back into the sterile coldness of the main house. "You're free to explore of course. I'll just show you the points of interest. All I ask is that you stay out of the locked areas."

Good on his word, he showed me the entrance for the gardens, the kitchens, the best lounges, and the pool before showing me to one of the guest rooms.

As I sat on the plush bed, oddly surprised by the comfort, I realized I wasn't nearly as anxious this time as I was when last separated from my mates. I knew they had each other, and even though death was sending them on an errand to do gods knew what, I didn't have that same fear I would never see them again. Was I scared shitless to be in Hades's halls alone? Sure. But I wasn't ready to break down or have a panic attack, and I'd take that as a win.

I'd never felt this powerful in my entire life. And it wasn't just because of the added abilities my mates had given me. They helped me feel confident. I could solve problems with my magic on the fly, discover new things and not have them go completely haywire. They grounded me. Provided a shelter I didn't even know I needed.

I huddled under the covers, the vetiver scent of the pillows lulling my eyelids closed, and I gave in to my exhaustion.

Sunlight was still streaming in the windows when I was roused by a knock at my door. The construct was on the other side, and I barely resisted recoiling. I'd traveled quite a ways with this creature, but I still couldn't get used to the bizarre construction. The flayed appearance of her lips, still red, raw, and glistening.

"Master Hades requested I check in on you. Do you require anything?" The mechanical voice issued from a mouth that hardly moved.

"No, thank you. I was just heading out to explore."

"Very good. Dinner will be in two hours. Master Hades requests that you attend. Wardrobe will be provided."

"Wardrobe?" I asked.

"Every dinner is a formal dinner. Your attire needs to be appropriate."

I blinked, taken aback. "Aren't I the only one here?"

Her head tilted to the side. "Master Hades doesn't need a crowd for a special occasion."

My face slipped into an annoyed mask before I realized he could probably see me through her eyes if he wished. I plastered a smile on my face. "Alright. I'll be there."

She bowed at the waist and walked away. I slipped out the door, shutting it behind me. Two hours to explore and plan an escape route while I was at.

Just in case.

The rest of the manor was much like what I'd already seen. I found a study and a library, all with very standard book options. It's always disappointing not to find mysterious grimoires or ancient texts when you're snooping around the house of a powerful god.

I traversed the main floor, where I'd arrived, certain I'd run into somebody. But everything was quiet. And for a formal dinner to be happening, the dining room was bare, not a single table setting in sight.

The kitchens in the far back of the house were empty as well. Shame. I was hoping to grab a little snack.

As I turned to leave, I noticed a door set into an alcove at the end of the hall. I tried the knob and it turned.

I cast a surreptitious glance around. Even though I'd been assured the only places off-limits were locked doors, it still felt like I wouldn't want to be caught here.

The door opened into a dark stairwell. I stood at the top, straining my ears to catch any sign of life down below. I didn't need gut instinct to tell me that the lord of the underworld might have some creepy things hiding in a basement.

When I tucked a strand of hair behind my ear, I paused as it brushed the pointed tip. It figured that the mate I took on a permanent physical change from was the one that might not want anything to do with me. I was fond of the look though.

The stairs immediately opened into a wider chamber that split into three separate hallways. I did a quick round of eenie, meenie, miney, moe before choosing the hallway to the left.

Small lamps burned intermittently, each one spaced at least twenty yards apart from the next. It provided just enough light for my night vision to function properly, a fact I was grateful for as another split appeared. I took the left fork again, figuring it would be easier to remember my path.

I looked over my shoulder, just to make sure there weren't any surprise forks I couldn't see that would get me hopelessly lost on the way back.

So far, there was nothing out of the ordinary. I still hadn't heard any movement, had seen nothing other than bare stone walls. I'd been traveling for long enough and needed to make it back in time for dinner, so I turned and headed back.

There were no surprises, and I returned to the initial chamber and stairway in good time. I was about to climb the stairs back to the main floor when I heard a small sound. It could've been movement, or even a whisper, but it faded so fast I couldn't tell. I took a few steps toward the tunnel on the far right and listened.

At the edge of my hearing, I could've swore I heard a small sob followed by a sniffle. A quick double-back to follow the sound, and I heard it again.

I froze, straining my ears. More sounds came, and I headed back into the main chamber. Now it sounded like they were issuing from the center hall.

How much time did I have left before someone came looking for me? As much as I wanted to explore further, I didn't want to anger my host, so I made the long walk back to my room to prepare for dinner.

CHAPTER TWO

Gareth

"Talk?" asked Felix. His immediate distrust of the nephilim was clear in the firm crossing of his arms over his chest. He stepped to the front of the group, still doing his utter best to avoid looking at Arthur's body.

"That's all," said Risha. "Meg is my friend."

I snorted. "She might've mentioned you a couple of times, but it was always in relation to how you stood by Belsioch, even when she was being kept in a cage and tortured."

Risha closed her eyes tight. When she opened them again, she avoided our gazes. "That was a mistake. For the record, I hated what was happening to her. I figured the faster I worked and made it possible for Bel to travel through time to" —she looked even more guilty now— "to capture you, the faster he would let her go. She *is* my friend. That's why I brought you here."

"I hate to be that guy," said Andrus, "but can we set Arthur down somewhere. Preferably somewhere cold?"

Risha faltered, stammering. "Uh, sure. Yes. We have a large refrigeration unit for my experiments."

After getting the body stored away, Risha invited us to have a seat. We all declined. "We need to be going, so make this quick" I said.

"How is Meg doing?" she asked. There was a genuine earnestness to her tone that loosened up my nerves a fraction.

I folded my arms across my chest. "As well as can be expected, given that we've been hunted by Hounds, imprisoned by your master, survived the eruption of Vesuvius—"

"My villa didn't," Felix grumbled.

"I'm sure it's still there, it just might look a little different when they uncover it two thousand years in the future," said Andrus.

Felix shot him a look but left it at that.

"But other than all those things," said Risha, her voice small. She'd cast her eyes down, and her shoulders hunched in on themselves bit by bit as I listed but a fraction of the obstacles we'd faced.

"So once again. Why did you bring us here?" I asked.

"We have a mutual enemy."

Andrus looked at her, eyebrows raised in mock incredulity. "Did you finally figure out that Belsioch is an asshole?"

"It's not just that," she said, annoyed at the implication. "I've hated him for a long time. But my brother was fiercely loyal. Even after Bel turned on him, it took my brother a while to see what a monster he was. Once I got him free from here, I turned my sights against Bel."

Andrus scoffed. "You were the one that provided him the means to travel through time. And I'm assuming you were the one who developed the trap that caught Death. That seems to be the opposite of working against him."

"No. Well, yes. I did do those things. But what Bel doesn't know is that I put safeguards in place along the way. That key that he's using to travel... we can hijack it anytime we want. I can disable it and trap him in whatever time he's in. Which, if I guess rightly, he's in medieval Paris right about now. About the time that you guys left."

"He's going after Legion?" asked Remi, his face darkening.

"I think so, yes. When the Hounds mentioned that battle, and leaving Legion in tatters, there was a keen interest on Bel's part. I can't know what his plans are for sure when he finds Legion, but it won't be anything good for us."

"I take it you need something from us?" I asked.

Risha lifted her chin, her confidence returning. "I wanted to talk with you about the Titans. Get answers directly from the people involved. That know them best."

"And this pertains to the issue with Belsioch, how?" asked Felix.

"I'm getting there," said Risha, waving him off.

Felix was about to say something else, but Remi clamped a hand on his shoulder. He'd been getting more restless as this meeting went on, casting glances back at the refrigerator, where Arthur's body was lying.

Risha noted the interaction before asking, "Am I to take it that Meg is onboard with releasing the Titans?"

We all nodded. "It didn't take much convincing after she found out Belsioch's true motives."

Risha shrugged. "That can't be helped."

"And your stance on the matter?" I asked.

"I would love to see them stay locked away. But I also realize I have biases. What are their intentions when they get free?" she asked.

I blanched at that. "To be honest, we're not certain."

The nephilim's eyebrows shot up. "How can you not—"

Remi answered her. "We are certain that their intentions are the same as they've always been. Keeping a balance. Making sure that creatures like Belsioch can't abuse their power. I think they'll just prefer to fade away, once they're free. They want to be left alone, as they always have. They'll help where it's needed, but otherwise, I don't think we'll hear too much from them."

"That seems a bit anti-climactic. You'll forgive me if I don't believe that."

It was Remi's turn to shrug. "Believe it or not, it makes no difference to me. This is what I know. What I know of them and their motivations. They have no desire for world dominance. There might be a bit of a dustup as they deal some long-deserved justice. But they have no plans to enslave humans or Strangers. That was always something people like your master preferred."

Risha pursed her lips, deciding on his veracity. "I hope you appreciate what a difficult decision this is for me. I've devoted my entire life to Bel's cause. My parents raised me to believe that the Titans were the ultimate evil."

I widened my stance. "Belsioch twisted Meg's mind to make her think the same thing. But now she sees the truth. She's been there, you know. To Tartarus."

She spluttered. "What? How?"

"Plans gone awry," I said, and left it at that. "She saw what kind of horror they were living in. The monstrous things that Belsioch puts them through on a daily basis. She could barely speak when she returned, she was so horrified by what she saw.

Could you leave anybody in that kind of state? No matter how much you hated them? I can't say I would even wish that on Belsioch."

Andrus growled. "I'd much prefer to see him dead."

There were general nods of agreement all around.

A smile quirked the corner of her mouth. "Did you know that Bel only imprisoned them because he couldn't destroy them?"

That caught me by surprise, and I wasn't the only one.

She nodded. "Only a god can kill a god, but Titans are on a whole different level. They can destroy the Ætherim, but the opposite is not true. Neither he, nor any of his brethren have enough power to destroy the kind of energy the Titans possess." She grinned. "Maybe you can put this information to good use."

"So his only goal is to keep them locked away because he can't do anything else?"

She hesitated before answering that one. "He can, once all of the links to them are destroyed. That's why he's been hunting you. After you and Meg are out of the way, he can just wear them down until there's not enough linking them to the outside world. They'll fade, and then he can kill them. That was his plan all along. The slow game. He would've been happy leaving them there to rot for eternity, if it weren't for their last-ditch effort for freedom when they created Meg."

"Is that what he told you? Don't forget that the Fates had no small role in this," said Remi. "It was always meant to come down to a final battle between him and the Titans. After Prometheus's betrayal, it cost them. They chose to imprison themselves. The Titans who died sacrificed themselves so their brethren would have enough power to get them through.

"Time was the only thing that would remedy the situation. It was a waiting game from the beginning. And only fate and luck have a hand in deciding when that final confrontation will take place. Guiding everything to a culmination at just the right point."

"Well, then what are we even doing here?" asked Risha, attempting to lighten the moment and hide her discomfort. "Fate has it under control."

"And if that pesky free will didn't get in the way, I'd agree with you," said Remi.

Risha nodded. "I suppose so." There was a long stretch of silence, and I thought Felix was going to lose his mind. He was pacing back and forth now, eager to get back to Death. Eager to get his best friend back.

"So about Belsioch?" Felix asked, finally snapping.

The nephilim blinked. "Right—"

A static noise in the corner of the room caught our attention right before the Hounds appeared, looking haggard.

The four of us moved into a defensive formation. "What the hell are they doing here?" asked Remi.

The Hounds finally focused their eyes on us and realized who we were. But instead of coming after us, they scoffed. "We aren't here for you," said the female. "The contract on you has been officially canceled. We've got a bigger problem."

"What happened?" asked Risha.

"Bel. He's combined himself with Legion. Into a single entity."

CHAPTER THREE

Bel

Legion didn't stand a chance against me. They fought. Tried to maintain autonomy. But in their weakened state my will absorbed and usurped theirs. I stood in that chamber, arms raised, letting every drop of Legion's power pour into me. I drained the last vestiges of the magick they'd wrought underneath this cathedral. The grass beneath my feet withered and died, and the stone altar split with a deafening crack.

The obsidian shadow that crowded the edges of the chamber drew back with a scream and returned to the hell that spawned it. As each torch lining the wall flickered and died, I grew more powerful still. I dug down deep into the recesses, the foundation of the foundations, and I took it all. Every ounce of power that Legion ever possessed was mine.

I felt whole again, vitality coursing through me like it did in my prime on the battlefields. The last torch guttered out and I was left in pitch darkness. Except it wasn't.

My body was glowing, black flame dancing off my skin. I held my hands in front of me, marveling. Legion was still there. I could feel the multiple vessels that they called bodies writhing and wanting to split off from me, act independently, even though they were a part of me.

Because we were one. A single entity. A hybrid of chaos and madness, cruelty and malice. Power was mine again.

I roared with victory, my voice filling the air until it rang off the walls. The earth trembled beneath my feet with each step I took. I climbed the stairs and as I entered the rectory, bodies were scattered across the floor. They must've been tied to Legion. I stepped over a cowled man, fallen on his way to pray at the altar, his hand outstretched asking for one final salvation. But it would never come.

The people in the town square cowered as they watched me descend the stairs with blatant fear in their eyes, pulling their children close and averting their gazes as I swept by. Several crossed themselves and I grinned. A woman and two small brats were frozen in terror, the mother whispering prayers under her breath. I gave her a toothy smile and a nod, and the pathetic thing passed out, dropping straight down in a heap.

I moved along with a delighted laugh as her children screeched, already formulating the many ways I could now exact my revenge.

Somewhere in the back of my mind I registered a portal opening, but thought nothing of it. The sun was going down and before the night was over, I wanted to create an urban legend in this city that they would fear all the way to modern times.

What would be best? Slaughter? Torture? Just make people disappear off the face of the earth? A nice melange of all three?

The city was coming alive, the underbelly and all the filth that hid there slinking onto the streets as the shadows lengthened. I came across a small group of humans, already drunkenly swaying through the alleys.

Too easy.

What else? Ah. Guards at the end of their shifts at the armory, looking for company with the ladies painted thick with makeup. That had potential to make a splash. Scandal, sex, horror, everything a good spree needs to become legendary.

I let my power well to the surface, testing it out, becoming familiar. Absorbing Legion had restored the majority of my godly ability, but there were new features there that I looked forward to exploring further.

The group I was stalking had no idea what was coming for them. I followed them to a dark alley where they thought to secret themselves away. The shadows were deep enough to hide within, and I decided to let them get started, to make the attack more unexpected and hilarious.

But something pulled at me, another presence watching. Reluctantly, I turned away from my intended victims and stepped out onto the main street. Just ahead of me were standing three figures, the forms of which I knew on sight.

The Hounds.

"What brings you here?" I asked. "Come to finish off what was left of Legion?"

They said nothing and I drew closer, unafraid. "Or were you just in the mood to visit this shithole and bask in the human waste?" My lip curled in disgust.

"What have you done, Belsioch?" asked the female. One of these days I should learn their names properly.

"Improved my circumstances," I answered with a casual shrug of my shoulder. "Can't blame a man for that."

"How did you manage it?" asked the short fellow. A small thrill went through me as I realized there was a hint of fear in his voice.

"Manage what?" I asked, playing dumb.

"You should've both been destroyed in the attempt at merging," said the tall one.

"Yet here I stand before you." I laughed. "Would you just like to bow at my feet now, or will I have to force the matter?"

All three of them growled in unison, taking a menacing step forward. The gesture lost its punch when it was coordinated, more like choreography than the opening salvo to a battle.

"You really want to do this?" I asked, offering them one more chance.

They continued to stalk forward, and I laughed, excited. The sound put a hitch in their steps, but they carried on. "I've been waiting for a chance to test out my new abilities." My laughter turned dark. "This will be fun."

I rushed them, closing the distance between us and hammering them with a blast of energy that sent them flying back several paces. They landed on their feet, shaking it off as their forms changed, shifting and growing until three massive beings were standing in front of me, slavering and hungry for blood.

Anyone still on the streets shrieked and ran for cover.

Whenever a god relaxes the hold they have on their human form, it's somewhat an experience of nirvana. You're returning home to your natural body. As I shed the pathetic human skin, I soon towered over the buildings around us, and over the Hounds as well.

Power crackled as they drew more, building up their size to match mine until we must've been a semblance of a campy monster movie from the '50s.

They launched at me in a coordinated attack, hitting me from all sides, but it was no more than a minor annoyance. One of them landed a hit right in my kidney, and I stumbled back a pace with a hiss of pain. I threw off the other two and grabbed the man around the throat, clamping down hard on his windpipe.

He choked, thick, dark liquid spilling from his lips between jagged teeth. His claws raked my face, but the cuts barely bled before they were healed. I smashed him down into the ground, leaving a crater around him, forming my hand into a spade shape and stabbing down into his stomach.

The other two were on me before I could pull out his guts. Teeth latched into my shoulder, and I howled, striking backward and nailing the Hound in the face. Claws and teeth dug at me, tearing and rending. I flung them off again, putting some distance between us before I tapped into Legion's powers.

It was the oddest sensation, the feeling of being split. It wasn't painful as much as it was difficult to wrap my mind around. The more I focused on the "why's and "how's" of it happening, the slower the magick reacted. So I just let go. Two separate bodies formed outside of mine, wavering before they snapped into being.

The Hounds froze and my lips curled into a smile. They exchanged a single glance, before disappearing in a snap. I laughed, triumphant. They would rather run than face their demise. They were afraid of me.

This day couldn't get much better. I let myself shrink back to a normal human size, taking that form back with reluctance.

A sudden tickling sensation, like I'd stepped onto a hill of ants, rushed over my body before the time travel focus around my neck heated to a blistering temperature, bursting into flame.

I wrenched it off my neck and threw it down, watching as it melted into nothing. Risha. She must've made a master key, a failsafe.

Of course she did.

The bellow that tore from me shook the surrounding houses and I threw a blast of energy in all directions that leveled every building on the block. I stood in the middle of the cloud of dust and detritus, seething. I was cut off. She'd trapped me here.

She had no idea, none, what hell I would rain down upon her. My mind scrambled for a solution. There's no way some worthless nephilim was going to keep me from fulfilling my purpose. From attaining my goal.

She thought she was smarter than me, but I would show her. I dug around in Legion's memories, looking for something that would be useful. The demon was barely hanging on, their consciousness almost completely absorbed by mine. It wouldn't take much longer before they were completely a part of me and under my total control.

Legion wasn't the only chaos demon around. Maybe they had a sympathetic link to others. It only took a small bit of searching to find it.

I latched on, sending out a call to any and all that could hear it, hoping one of them would answer. After a long, still silence, something happened. A swirling vortex appeared in front of me, a beacon, calling to me and offering salvation.

I stepped through it.

CHAPTER FOUR

Meg

Dinner had been an awkward, quiet affair. The food was delicious, but the majority of the conversation was just odd. Most of the time my host would just ramble about nothing in particular, getting distracted easily, and going off on tangents before coming back to the main point. If he'd been trying to convince me that he was of sound mind, he didn't do a very good job of it.

I was more determined than ever to get out of here, and I solidified plans on my way back to my room. There were several exits out. None of them were blocked, and I hadn't been forbidden from leaving the grounds. Hades had eyes and ears all over this place, so he probably wasn't concerned that I'd be able to disappear.

There were spirits active in the halls now and that, at least, made me feel better. It had been too quiet. Not having a multitude of ghosts surrounding you at all times in a place like this felt wrong.

When I entered my room, a spirit was already turning down my bedsheets. She gave me a polite nod before she disappeared.

I hummed appreciatively. "Ghostly turn-down service. Farah should add that to her list of offerings."

I had nothing in the way of night clothes, so I settled for stripping down to my underwear before climbing into bed, and I drifted off, preparing for whatever the next day would bring.

When I woke, I was shivering. I looked around me in confusion, realizing I was standing in the dungeon chamber. In my underwear. In the cold and dark.

Not an ideal situation.

Once I was fully awake, I heard that terrified cry again, the same short sniffling sobs that had eluded me earlier.

Could this be a trap? Death had warned me about this place, and while there wasn't a "Welcome to My Dungeon" sign anywhere, it seemed like a safe assumption that this was exactly that.

A different kind of chill stole through me and I shivered. I wrapped my arms around my torso, digging my fingers into my skin. I drew the stone armor that I'd received from Remi to the surface.

It was much easier to draw each particular gift into use now. It only took a hundred years and four mates for me to figure out my magick. Mostly.

I crept down the passageway, sticking close to the wall. There was an odd rasping noise as my hardened skin scraped against the stone.

The cries still seemed to come from up ahead, so I carried on.

"Will you shut up? You should be used to being prisoner. This isn't much different than you're normal every day life."

I froze. It was Hades's voice, but it sounded... off.

"They'll kill you when they discover what you've done."

"But how are they going to find out?" he asked with a chuckle. "Are you going to tell them? You're never getting out of here. Now hush."

The woman lapsed into silence, but I could still hear her terrified breathing coming in gasps as she attempted to get herself under control.

"Better. Just answer my question, and I will leave."

"I was never told. You'd have to ask him."

"But I'm not asking him. You expect me to believe he wouldn't give you access?"

"That's actually the most believable thing of this whole situation," she snapped, once again finding her courage.

There was a loud smack, and she yelped. My fists clenched and I had to restrain myself. It was clear she was being held against her will, but it wouldn't do either of us any good if I just barged in there without knowing what I was walking into.

"Think long and hard," said Hades. "I'll be back in the morning."

"My answer will be the same."

He growled, and I heard heavy footsteps before a door opened. I attempted to pull the cloak of illusion around myself that I'd gained from Felix, but it wouldn't come. I cursed. Clearly, I didn't have as much of a handle on this as I thought.

There was no time to think about what I was doing wrong. The door clanged and I hurried back down the hall toward the chamber. I made it up the stairs and saw the door was open. Did I leave it that way when I slept walked down here, or had he left it that way? Would he notice? He'd notice.

I flipped a mental coin and chose to close the door, retreating into the kitchen and ducking into a closet just as I heard the door creak open again.

When I couldn't hear the footsteps anymore, I ventured out of my hiding place, creeping into the main part of the house, and back to my room, only allowing myself to breathe deeply once I was safe behind my own closed door.

Too terrified to go back to sleep, not knowing where I might wake up, I dressed and sat in the most uncomfortable position I could until the sun came up.

"Did you sleep well?" asked Hades at the table the next morning. His creepy servant had knocked on my door the same as yesterday to announce breakfast. Luckily, I didn't have to dress up for this one.

"Wonderfully, thank you. Very comfortable accommodations."

He inclined his head. "I'm glad to hear it. I only ask because the circles around your eyes seem darker than yesterday." He raised his eyebrows. "Is that normal for you?"

My heartbeat stuttered, but there was no way he could know. Unless of course, he'd orchestrated my nighttime adventure himself.

"Stress," I said, with a painfully fake smile. "You know how it is."

His eyes narrowed just a bit at the corners. "Certainly." He took a bite of the mixed fruit doused in lime syrup. "Any plans for today?"

"Thought I'd wander a bit more. Maybe pay a visit to my old neighborhood." And get some closure.

"That sounds like a fine idea. I'm not sure if I mentioned it, but I'm hosting a masquerade tomorrow night. Since you're here, it would be absurd not to attend."

"A full masquerade?" I asked.

"I've already had them begin work on a costume for you. Stop by the tailor's before you leave for your adventuring."

"Parties aren't really my style..." I said, making a lame attempt at declining.

"I'm sure you've attended before, but they're so much better now. Give it a try."

"Of course. Thank you for the invitation," I said, keeping my annoyed groan on the inside. "And the tailor is where?"

"Roshanna will show you."

The construct appeared next to me out of nowhere and I jumped, which made Hades laugh. "She's rather catlike, isn't she? Sneaks up on you out of nowhere. She's a great hunter too. Not much escapes her, in case you were wondering."

"Good to know," I said, hoping I didn't look as unnerved as I felt. I finished the last bit of breakfast, wiped my mouth on my napkin, and stood. "If you'll excuse me."

Hades made a sweeping gesture with his hand, and I followed Roshanna.

Small talk with the construct wasn't really appealing, so I followed in silence. Down a small hallway, we stopped in front of a plain-looking door. Behind it, I could hear the clacking of a sewing machine, one of the old-fashioned ones with a hand wheel. My guide opened the door and ushered me into a room that took me by surprise. It was warm and brightly lit, the walls covered in a soft goldenrod. Sunlight streamed in the large windows overlooking a large workshop full of bolts of cloth, scraps of cut fabric littering the floor and workbenches, and entire racks of suits and dresses of breathtaking quality.

"This is the girl?" I hadn't even noticed the sewing machine had stopped and when I looked to the source of the voice, a kind-looking man with graying hair going white at the temples and a single shock of white in the front, was appraising me over his glasses. He got to his feet and bustled over, guiding me to a small, raised platform in the middle of the room. He instantly produced a measuring tape and ran it along my torso and legs. "Master Hades was quite close in his estimations. I'll only need to make a few adjustments."

He hurried off back to his workstation, flipping his hand absentmindedly toward a table on the far side of the room. "The available masks are over there. Choose one, and I'll add the details to your gown."

I took my time, examining the room as I made my way over to the display. An odd fondness came over me as I ran my hands across bolts of fabric. Satin, velvet, brocade, linen. All the highest quality and a feast of sensation. A closer inspection of the other gowns he made was in order. I cast a glance at him, just to make sure I wasn't stepping on his toes, but he didn't pay me any attention.

The detail on the first rack of dresses I examined was incredible. Handsewn flowers with tiny beads for accent, delicate gold piping, jewels. I found things like this ostentatious and off-putting. But this man made it an artform. Beauty without excess. If this is what he normally produced, I was looking forward to seeing what he was making for me.

The masks were all the typical affair that you would see at a masquerade. Cloth-covered half-masks that covered your eyes and nose, supported by a stick. There were a few that banded around the head. But one stuck out.

I reached out carefully, like I was afraid it would come to life.

The ibis head reminded me of a plague doctor mask, except the beak was longer and thinner before it curved downward. The face was made with tiny black jewels shaped like feathers that sparkled in the light. A halo of silky, opalescent feathers lined the crown and cheeks.

"Excellent choice," said the tailor, from right over my shoulder. I jumped and whirled around. "Sorry dear, didn't mean to startle you." He tried to disguise the smile on his face. "I'll get started on the details right away."

I nodded dazedly and Roshanna motioned me toward the door.

"Some people say the original goal of masquerades was to embody the creature you emulated with your mask. A primal spirit. Some people think wearing a mask like this allows someone to tap into that energy." He shrugged. "Just a thought."

"It certainly does give you something to think about. Thank you."

He bowed his head and went back to his work.

And I went to visit what was left of my old life.

CHAPTER FIVE

Meg

The weather was the same mild warmth it always was in this city. The sun shone brightly but Hades must've been feeling some kinda way since a hot breeze was blowing through the streets. It whipped around corners and bounced off the city walls.

As I entered the gates to the district where my old "home" sat—Roshanna was trailing far behind this time, so I had a chance to experience my surroundings rather than be focused on the creepy construct accompanying me—I was struck with a sense of melancholy.

When I was a little girl and hadn't yet become the stubborn, discontented problem child, I'd been allowed to sit at the window. There weren't many other children, but I would watch them from my upstairs playroom as they ran around, wishing I could play, too.

The Gieses thought that if they gave me a nanny to keep me quiet and shoved me in a room by myself for hours at a time (with toys that wouldn't hold any child's interest for long), it would be enough.

Those years were so painfully lonely.

And now the streets were almost empty. A few servants scurried along, heads bowed against the wind, but there were no other signs of life. I waited until Roshanna caught up to me. "What happened here? Where is everyone?"

She looked at me with her blank expression before her lips moved, out of sync with her words. I was getting used to it, but it still gave me chills. "They keep to their houses, mostly."

"Why? It used to be a lively city." I pulled a face at the unintended irony. "All things considered."

The construct nodded. "Used to be, yes. People are leaving for other realms. A few have wandered off into the wastelands, looking to join the dead. When the Gieses were attacked, it scared the other families. Especially powerful ones. They'd always felt untouchable. But Belsioch proved that wasn't true. They weren't safe in their hideaways, separated from the other realms and protected by Master Hades. So they retreated. Or left." Roshanna gazed around and an almost sentient expression crossed her face for an instant. "It is quiet now. The power is waning."

I nodded slowly, taking a deep breath before resuming determined steps toward the wreckage of the Giese's manor. The wind whistled through the charred skeleton of the structure, a strange keening that set my teeth on edge.

There was an air of loneliness about the place that was just as significant as the pall that constantly hung over me as a child. Charred timbers were piled in the middle of the collapsed structure and ash still stirred in the breeze.

"Why didn't they raze this property?" I asked.

"Master Hades saw it fitting to leave it as a reminder."

"A reminder of what? Wouldn't it be a testament of his failure to protect his own city?"

Roshanna shook her head, adamant. "No. It was a reminder of what would happen to those he chose not to protect."

I balked. "What do you mean by *chose*?"

Rosanna cocked her head. "Does that word not mean what I think it means?" She blinked. "He chose not to protect them. They were a thorn in his side for a long time. He never cared for their actions, but he couldn't do anything without appearing heavy handed. Nor did he want to risk angering the Titans. Bel did everyone a favor."

I hummed thoughtfully, finding a path through the wreckage to explore farther into the home. Some of the upper floors were still intact, although hanging on by a thread. Now that I was among the destruction, the acrid smell of smoke was still lingering. It was almost astringent whenever I kicked up a loose board, unleashing a puff of ash that hadn't been tampered with for fifty years.

There were some sticks of furniture discernible, the edges of gold gilt frames glinting whenever they caught the sun. I unearthed one, brushing it off with my hands as I lifted it free.

It had been a painting, some kind of abstract monstrosity that I never understood, but that they assured me was the epitome of fancy art. It always hung in the dining room, and I would stare at it resolutely, trying to make sense of it rather than listening to whatever ridiculous thing my foster family was going on about. You only needed to listen to them spout their self-serving nonsense once before you had heard the entire argument.

I moved to a spot that would've been right below my bedroom when the upper floors had collapsed. I didn't know what I was expecting to find, or even if I wanted to find anything, but I picked through the debris regardless.

Roshanna was wandering behind me, staring around aimlessly, occasionally brushing at a smudge of dirt that transferred onto her clothing.

I continued my searching and tried to make conversation, hoping I could slip in some questions and catch her off guard, getting her to answer a question she shouldn't.

"How long have you been working for Hades?" I asked.

Her eyes flicked to me only briefly before she went back to watching each carefully placed step as she found a path through with the least chance of getting dirty. "I'm not very good at telling time. It might've been a decade. It might've been a hundred years." She shrugged. "It doesn't matter to me. Serving Master Hades is an honor."

"Is this the majority of the work you do for him? Babysitting? Retrieving rogue travelers on the planes?" My toe kicked something and it went skittering. I chased after it to get a closer look, but found it was only a wooden bauble that had fallen off something.

Roshanna didn't respond immediately and I chanced a glance to see what she was thinking. She was staring at something in a gloomy corner, shadowed from the sunlight.

"Did you find something?"

Without taking her eyes off it—whatever it was—she motioned me over. As I neared her, she pointed. "Do you see that?"

I peered closer. There was something glinting, and I had to carefully skirt piles of shattered pottery and glass to get to it. Once I pulled the object free and realize what it was, I gasped.

A silver ring, made to fit over the thumb. It was shaped like a raven's claw, and I remembered in vivid detail all the times my foster mother had used it against me. She wore it always, would relish wrapping her hand around my arm, and digging the claw on her thumb into my skin, drawing just a thin trickle of blood.

Since she was always wearing it, I wondered...

"Can you help me lift this?" I asked Roshanna.

The construct nodded and stepped closer to grip the edge of a solid piece of fallen plaster that was still holding together remarkably well. With a concerted effort, we lifted it and leaned it back against the wall.

Underneath was more rubble, but something told me I should still sift through it. Gingerly, not wanting to risk slicing myself open on an unseen hazard, I dug down. It wasn't long before something bright white gleamed up from the ashes.

My heart pounded as emotions roiled to the surface. Empathy and compassion were not among them, but there was a certain degree of shock. I'd known they were dead, Bel had told me as much, and there was no reason not to believe him. But as I reached down and pulled Astrid Giese's skull from its impromptu tomb, it put a finalized point on everything from those years.

This woman had caused me nothing but torment. I was a tool, a status symbol. Something for her to use for her own gain. She was never a mother, never even a semblance of an evil stepmother. She was a horrible, vindictive woman, whose first reaction was violence whenever I dared to contradict her. Astrid always doled out the harshest punishment whenever I refused to be their puppet.

"Sit still."

"Keep silent."

"Smile."

The constant mantra that I heard nearly every day.

And now I was holding her bare skull in my hands. The fire had cracked the bone, and the ashes had bleached it. The mouth was open, the jaw twisted in a rictus of a scream. The urge to smile came over me, and I didn't stop it. I had hoped to find closure, and I felt more at peace in this moment than I had since I escaped this hell.

I dropped the skull back to the floor, tossed the ring after it, and shuffled back to Roshanna. I was done here.

Chapter Six

Gareth

"Combine with Legion? That's possible?" asked Felix.

The Hounds ignored the question. "He's something beyond what he was. They were both weak," the taller male said, shaking his head in disbelief. "But since they've combined..."

He didn't have to finish that sentence. I could see the fear in his eyes.

Risha rushed to her desk and grabbed what I thought was a paperweight, a heavy glass orb. She lifted it over her head and smashed it on the ground, power surging out of it in a flash before it dissipated. A focus.

"What did you just do?" Remi asked.

The nephilim spared him a glance before turning back to the shattered mess on the floor. "That was the failsafe. Assuming he's still in the time the Hounds left him in, he's trapped. Let's hope he didn't make it back to our time."

"And if he did?" asked Andrus.

The Hounds growled and gnashed their teeth.

"You're not used to losing," I said, finding some humor in the moment. It certainly made them less frightening.

Their eyes focused on me with sharp intensity. "We didn't lose."

"He's still alive," I said. Andrus glared daggers into the side of my head.

All three prowled over to us, circling like sharks. "Why do you antagonize us, wolf? Do you have a death wish?" the female asked.

"Or maybe you're just stupid," said the short one.

"Just because the contract on you is no longer valid, does not mean we will hesitate to cut you down," said the tall one. "Especially since you are working with Death."

The others sneered at the mention of the egregore.

"This changes things," said Risha. She was lost in thought, not at all aware that the Hounds were ready to pick a fight in the middle of her laboratory.

She walked right through the middle of our groups. "I was going to ask you to help me develop a plan to lure Bel into the open, so one of his *many* enemies could kill him. You'd make great bait. But now, that's not going to work. If we can't overpower him..."

"I think we're all in agreement that eliminating Belsioch is the best choice," said Felix. "We just need to figure out a different tactic."

I looked at Risha skeptically. "You're truly willing to help us? Even if that means the Titans will go free?"

She fell silent. "I'm willing to take the risk. Especially with this new"—she cleared her throat—"issue of Bel's abilities. I would dare say *he's* the biggest threat, not the Titans."

Her gaze swept off to the side and her mind traveled back to someplace none of us could see. "Meg trusts them." The nephilim considered before nodding her head in a sharp jerky motion. "I'm willing to see how things play out."

"Bold words to say when we're dealing with immensely powerful beings. Once they're free, you're never getting them back in that prison again," said Remi.

Andrus, Felix, and I all gave him the usual reproachful glare. "Meg will be glad to know that she has you back on her side." I glanced at the Hounds. "These ones I haven't quite figured out, though. Where do you stand on this?"

The Hounds we're trying to put on their usual façades of confidence, but it was still plain to see how shaken they were from their dustup with Belsioch.

"Belsioch will die, have no doubts. We were taken by surprise is all. Once we're properly prepared for an attack, we'll hunt him down ourselves. The lot of you can keep out of it," said the tall one.

Risha didn't care for that answer. "Are you sure that's wise?"

My eyes widened as I glanced between them. I don't know what her relationship was with them, but she seemed far too comfortable as a co-conspirator.

The Hounds stilled. A slight shift, the corners of their eyes tightened, their frowns drooped almost imperceptibly. They didn't care for being questioned, but there was something else there. Dare I say a sense of doubt?

She pushed away from the desk, crossing to a small closet, and pulling out a dustpan and broom. Seeing a nephilim doing common household chores threw me for a loop.

"If we formulate a plan as a team—" she began.

The female Hound scoffed. "*Team*? What kind of ridiculous notion is that? Who do you think you're talking to?"

"Beings that just got their asses handed to them."

They growled and took a menacing step forward but she held up her hand. "It wasn't meant as an insult. Are you really going to deny that's what happened?"

"We don't lose," said the squat male.

"There's a first time for everything," said Risha, tone hard.

They exchanged glares and then the Hounds disappeared.

When it seemed certain they weren't coming back, I said, "Do you trust them?"

She leaned back against the desk. "I was horrified when I learned that Bel had sent them after you. I was worried sick about Meg. But they are actually quite honorable. Terrifying, but..."

Andrus snorted. "Have you ever seen them transform? Because if you haven't, that's an eye-opener. You don't know terrifying until you've seen that."

Risha shuddered. "I haven't. Hopefully I never will. But if you have their word on something, you can trust them to keep it. And if they have no contract against you, unless you really anger them, there's no reason you shouldn't be safe from them. They operate in a very black-and-white manner. I'd rather work with them than half the other people I know. Even if they could kill me in the blink of an eye, I trust they won't."

"Do you still need anything from us? I think we could all agree that we will help you destroy Belsioch if we can, but we need to go," said Felix.

"We're good here," said Risha. "I just wanted to take your temperature. Meg seems like she's in good hands."

"You don't know the half of it," said Remi, the hint of a smile on his face.

Andrus and I could do nothing but stare at the gargoyle in shock, and all of Felix's jitters came to screeching halt as he gaped in disbelief.

"Did you just make a joke?" Andrus asked.

Remi's smile became a bit more devilish, but he said nothing.

Felix fought back a laugh as he clapped him on the shoulder. "Thank you for that, my friend."

"How should I contact you?" asked Risha.

My companions looked to me expectantly. Why would they think I would know how to communicate across timelines?

But as soon as I had that thought, another came to mind as Time spoke to me. Flashes of wordless thought, images, *knowing*. I reached up and took one of the warrior rings out of my beard and handed the small piece of iron to Risha. As I gave her the instruction, it almost felt as if someone else was speaking through me.

"Use this as a focus. If you have one of your time-travel-imbued items on hand it will be easier. When this gets hot, you'll know you've made a connection. Then speak. I should hear you."

She nodded and pocketed the ring. "Thank you." She bowed her head to the group. "I'm glad we had a chance to speak. You've given me a lot to think about."

"If we can indeed count on you as an ally," I said, "Meg will be glad to hear it."

The nephilim gave me a small smile and led the way back to the refrigeration unit where we collected Arthur's body.

"Have we figured out how we're getting a hold of Death?" Andrus asked.

Without missing a beat, Felix yelled into the open air. "Death! We've got him! Come get us!"

We waited. I could tell Remi was about to give Felix a smartass reply, but a portal popped open in the middle of our group.

"On we go," said Felix, motioning us forward.

I gave a brisk nod to Risha, and we stepped through the portal.

CHAPTER SEVEN

Felix

"Where are we?" asked Andrus. "This isn't New Orleans, is it?"

We'd blinked back into existence and Death with standing and waiting for us, arms crossed and tapping her foot impatiently. A perfect picture of comical reticence.

"Why is it that whenever I try to track any of you down, you're never in the same spot that I left you?" she asked. Her voice was smoky and alluring and it still threw me to hear it. She looked far too much like a paramour from my past, one things hadn't ended well with. As she moved toward us, her curvy hips rolled in a tight-fitting dress. I'm sure there were many deep-seated issues that would point to why Death appeared to me like this, but I wasn't touching that with a ten-foot pole.

I always joked that that woman would be the death of me, but I never expected it to take such a literal turn. The most unsettling thing was that, where I remembered long summer days, struck by the way the sun glinted off the purple sheen of her hair and made her dark skin shine like gold, Death's version of her had a sickly pallor. It was almost a mockery of her beauty.

"In our defense, we thought you were the one that opened that first portal. If a doorway appears hovering in mid-air, I'm gonna walk through it," I said with a shrug. I glanced at our odd surroundings. "Where did you bring us?"

"You're in my home. It's the only place I can be sure to contain Arthur's soul without interference."

"Contain?" Remi asked.

Death ignored him, grimacing. "We might have to do a bit of triage on that thing," he said, giving a keen once over to Arthur's limp body suspended between my brothers. My vision narrowed in on Arthur's hand, the fingers on his left the only unmarred part of his body. Soaked in blood and obviously broken, but by far the easiest to look at without a wrenching pain that hit too close.

I think being separated from these men, especially Arthur, was the reason I so easily dissociated from my old life. It was just easier. As much as I would like to pretend that I didn't need anyone, being in their presence again proved that I did.

Death motioned for us to follow, and I looked around curiously at the place she called home. It all seemed relatively modest. There were no grand entryways or staircases, no golden gleam from every surface. Even the floors were simple, polished wood.

We walked through a short hall into a dining room that would only seat about ten people. Through the other side was a parlor of about the same size with comfortable furniture and a few simple pieces of art.

"How is this going to work?" asked Andrus. He paused. "Where's Meg?"

The rest of us looked around curiously, expecting her to walk in, flipping her hair over her shoulder with a confident smile like she always did. But she didn't appear.

"There's good news, and there's bad news." Death fixed us all with a severe look. "Meg was able to shove Arthur's soul through the portal, but she was detained at the last minute by one of Hades's constructs."

"What?" Gareth lurched forward, clenching his fists at his sides. "And you did nothing?" A barely restrained growl rumbled in his throat, and I saw his skin shiver as his wolf threatened to take over.

Death stared him down without any sign of concern. "I already warned her that I could not interfere."

"How would it have been interfering?" Andrus demanded. "All you had to do was jump in and pull her out."

The withering glare that Death delivered almost made *me* back up a step. Andrus's mouth snapped shut.

"That's all I had to do? I'm glad you think politics are so simple between the gods." An eerie light glinted in her eyes as she fixed her gaze on each of us. "I don't think any of you understand just how delicate of a situation we are in now. We obviously need to send a rescue for your mate. But Hades has not been the same for a long time, he's unpredictable." She paused and huffed. "More unpredictable than usual. I thought that you would at least be able to figure out the importance that he and I be able to continue to work together. Our professions do cross over." She snorted. "Get it? Cross? Over?"

I gave her a complimentary laugh just to fill the *dead* air... get it?

She took a breath. "None of this will be simple."

My mind was already racing. How much danger was Meg in? Fear wormed into my gut.

"So what are we supposed to do?" Remi asked.

"For starters, you can set that body over there." Death pointed to a corner that appeared empty to my eyes, but Remi gasped.

I looked at him. "What's wrong?"

Remi blinked hard, still staring into the corner as he and Andrus brought Arthur's body over and laid it down. Remi back away, his eyes never leaving a point midway up the wall.

Andrus was looking in the same direction, but his focus didn't seem quite so honed.

"What are you looking at?" Gareth asked, tone sharp. A grin tugged at the corner of my mouth. He always hated unknowns, especially when he was in the presence of one.

Andrus wrenched his eyes away, sparing a glance at Gareth before turning his attention back to Remi. "Do you see him too?"

Remi nodded. "It's a carbon copy of him, but gray." His voice was hushed, almost reverent.

"All I see is a hazy outline, but I can tell it's him."

Gareth put it together before I did. "Arthur's soul is there?"

The two of them nodded and I relaxed a bit. Ghosts I could handle. "What's he doing?" I asked.

Andrus looked at Remi to explain. "He's just staring at his body. He looks so sad and confused."

Death sighed. "An unfortunate side effect. We're going to need to give him time to process what he's looking at. When Meg shoved him through, the majority of his memories were gone, if there were any left at all."

"So without her here, how are we going to restore him? Is he just going to go back to normal once he reenters his body?" I asked.

Death shook her head. "No. He can't leave my house, so we don't have to worry about the underworld calling him back. But all we can do is wait for him to adjust. The hope is he'll reenter his body on his own. He does recognize himself at least. But anything else..." She chewed her lip. "There's no way to restore him as he was, not without Meg. He'll be like a child again. He'll know basic functions; nobody is going to have to do diaper duty. But his mind will be blank. A clean slate."

"Who's going after her?" Gareth asked, always the first one to jump into the fray.

"I am hesitant to suggest that any of you go." Death held up her hand to silence Gareth's objections. "But we have no choice. I would suggest at least two of you go on this journey. You'll be more able to keep each other from losing yourselves to the inherent dangers the living face in the underworld."

"Why is it that dangerous though? There are other living beings that reside in the underworld. There are several Æther-im, a couple of noble families. Some of my dark fae brethren prefer to spend their time there." I shrugged. "Is this just a cautionary thing? Dependent upon how hardy of a person you are?"

Death's sigh was almost identical to the ones I'd hear from the lover whose face she wore when said lover was ready to kill me. "By all means, why don't you fae-splain this to me?" She popped her hip to the side and clicked her nails dangerously. "The gods know I'm a novice at all this. What can I possibly educate you on?"

"Point taken," I said, holding up my hands.

"This will be difficult enough for whoever goes over there just dealing with Hades. But if you make it out—which I'm not doubting you will—you could very well wind up with a lingering side effect. Your soul might always be restless. Wanting you to return to the underworld. If you don't have a strong enough anchor, there's a good likelihood that at some point you'll decide to return. And the most expedient way to get there is the old-fashioned way."

"Meg could also get us in," Remi pointed out. "Or you."

Death pinched her nose between her eyes. "Must you always insist on being *that guy*?" She glared. "If you weren't a package deal, I would rescind the offer to all of you and just take Meg for my team."

Gareth's unease was plain as he flicked his eyes toward me. While I still wasn't fully onboard since I hadn't been offered the *choice* to join this little cabal of theirs, I was warming up to the idea. I didn't relish the thought of being left behind again while the rest of my brothers in arms, my family, gallivanted around the world without me.

And as much as I was hesitant to admit it, Meg was increasingly on my mind. I'm sure right about now she would've been giving me side eye, hand anchored on her hip while she waited for a smartass remark.

"It goes without saying that I volunteer to take the trip," said Gareth. "I don't think maintaining my anchor to this world will be a problem. I have her."

"I volunteer as well," said Andrus and Remi at the same time.

I rolled my eyes. "Are you trying to make me look bad?" I said the words with a light tone.

Death watched the three of them with a mixture of amusement and disgust at their saccharine display of love. "I never thought I'd be a fan of the side effects of lovesick infatuation, but in this case, it seems to be working in our favor."

"She's calling you all a bunch of lovesick fools," I said.

"She?" asked Death, her annoyance turning to intrigue in a flash. "Who do I look like to you?"

The others were all watching me, and I tried not to fidget. "An ex," I said, reluctant to share that small amount of personal information. I stared at the floor, intent on working a knot from my neck. "You don't know her."

Death's lips curved in a teasing smile and a thin black eyebrow peaked in a perfect V. "Interesting."

"It's not. Let's continue with the important discussion, please."

I could already tell I wasn't hearing the end of it so easily.

"Someone will need to stay here with Arthur," she continued. "Once he's back in his body, he'll be free to roam, and I won't be able to keep an eye on him 24/7."

My eyes crept back over in Arthur's direction, half-hoping and half-dreading to see his soul reanimate his ghoulish body.

"I think that's a job I'm much better suited for anyway," I said. "Otherwise, we'll draw far too much attention from my ravishing good looks."

Remi frowned, his wings rustling. "Or we could just send you alone and it would be tantamount to sending three people right there. You, yourself, and your ego."

"When do we leave?" asked Gareth.

"As soon as Arthur's soul returns to his—"

A gasping breath rattled from dead lungs, and I flinched.

Death frowned. "Oh. Uh... I thought that would take longer." She waffled back and forth before holding up her index finger. "Give me a sec."

She crossed over to Arthur and leaned down as the body spasmed, flailing necrotic limbs starting to purple and bruise since we removed him from that hellish time capsule. I forced myself to watch as she leaned down and whispered something in his ear, her dark hair pooling on the floor.

The body stilled and she placed her hand on his forehead, a soft light pulsing around him.

"What's happening?" asked Gareth, keeping his voice low.

Remi was watching the whole thing with unveiled awe. "Arthur's soul dissolved into the body. All I can see is this spectral mist around him now, flashing with little lights.

The body healed as we watched on and I sucked in a breath as Arthur finally opened his eyes. There was a heaving silence as we waited.

And then he screamed. Howling, anguished screams.

I didn't even realize I was moving until I was kneeling next to him, grabbing him up and crushing him to me in an embrace. "You're safe." I spoke into his ear, a mantra that I kept repeating until he began to quiet.

After long minutes, Death still working at healing his visible wounds, Arthur's arms hung limp at his sides, and I lowered him back down to the floor.

"Is he asleep?" asked Andrus.

"Yes," I said, fighting down the bile that tried to work its way up my throat. Without looking at Death, I asked, "What was that about?"

Death stood, staring down at the body with a hardened expression. "Small side effect." She shrugged helplessly. "There are just so many discordant things happening. The body and mind... it's a lot to reconcile."

"You seem shaken," said Remi.

She gave him a rueful smile. "I take souls. It's not often I put them back in their bodies."

A hand clasped my shoulder as I continued to stare down at Arthur. I looked up to find Gareth's sorrowful face.

"He'll be in good hands with you watching over him," he said. "And then Meg will bring him back, good as new."

CHAPTER EIGHT

Meg

Picking through the wreckage was useless. Anything I might've hoped to retrieve had been incinerated or stolen. No great loss.

"I think I'm ready to head back," I said, and Roshanna nodded.

I took the back way out of the house, wanting to see what was left of the gardens. Those had been my favorite growing up. Even when the Gieses kept me locked away when I was older, I could still see the gardens from my room. There couldn't have been much left.

We passed through the servant's quarters. It had been far less damaged in the fire, and the majority of it still stood. The floors in the main parts of the house had been stone, withstanding the fire just fine, but back here they were wood.

After a few tentative steps, I was confident they were sound enough to hold our weight, and I made my way quickly across. Roshanna followed. I was about to head through the back door when a loud crack made me turn. She had fallen partway through a hole in the floor, catching herself and seeming entirely unperturbed, even though half her body was hanging over empty air.

She held her hand out to me and I took careful steps back, testing each spot before I put my full weight into it. I braced myself and grabbed her hand, lifting her out of the hole.

"Thank you," she said, dusting herself off again. She was meticulous about cleanliness, picking at each offending splinter that still clung to her dress.

"I don't remember there being a basement here," I said, peering over into the hole. I couldn't see more than a foot into the darkness. "Can you summon light?" I asked Roshanna.

"Yes," she said, forming an orb of light and letting it float into the hole. It descended until it found the bottom. I lay flat on the floor, and stuck my head down beneath the boards.

"Holy shit," I breathed.

It was some kind of chamber—which seemed to be a common fixture around these parts—stone walls with arches tooled into them that resembled elaborate doorways.

Roshanna moved up beside me and peered down, seeming genuinely curious. "Do you know what this place is?" I asked, only taking my eyes briefly from the strange sight.

"No," she said. "It is odd. I've never even heard stories of this being here, and people have been exploring these ruins since shortly after the fire."

"No doubt trying to find all the treasures the Gieses hid away. They weren't quiet about their wealth, that's for sure."

"So I've heard. And yes, the other families picked this place pretty clean. Except, apparently, for the bodies." There was a tone of disapproval in Roshanna's voice. Maybe I was just projecting, but it seemed like she was becoming more open, more real, like Hades wasn't controlling her every move right now.

"Should we go down there?" I asked.

She looked at me, somewhat dubious. "I'm not sure that Master Hades would approve. I'm supposed to keep you safe."

"He doesn't have to know. And are you supposed to keep me safe, or just stop me from running away?"

She huffed a laugh. "You wouldn't get very far if you tried to run from me."

"Okay then, it's decided. Let's find a way down."

That emotionless mask slipped back over her face as she calculated the risk. After a long moment of thought, a mischievous grin twisted her mouth. "Alright."

I wrapped my stone skin around myself before I dangled over the edge of the abyss, kicking my feet into empty air and dropping down. I ended the fall in a light thump and a burst of dust that jumped around me in a torrent. Roshanna followed me, without any of the hesitancy that I'd shown, landing a lot harder and covering us both with more billowing dust.

I coughed, fanning my hand in front of my face until I could breathe again.

"This is unbelievable," I said, staring around me in fascination. Through the dust on the floor, I could vaguely see more patterns etched into the stone. "Is this some kind of portal room?"

Roshanna didn't answer, and I turned to find her staring at one of the doorways. I stepped closer, studying the design she seemed taken with.

The outlines were crisper than the others and there was a faint haze hovering in the air around it, a small amount of still active magick. I traced the delicate designs with my fingers and got zapped with what felt like static electricity.

"Ouch!" I said, stepping back and shaking my hand out. My fingers had gone numb and my blood felt like it was vibrating.

"What?" asked Roshanna, touching my shoulder. Whatever happened to me transferred to her, and the construct made an odd, garbled noise, something halfway between an animalistic cry and pure shock. She collapsed and I rushed to her side.

"Are you okay? What happened?"

Her eyes were closed, so I peeled the lids back, intending to check for any sign of... well, I guess I didn't really know what. But when I looked into her eyes, all I could do was stare.

They looked so human. The color had returned to a normal shade of brown and within them, I could see a truly human consciousness staring back.

"Roshanna?"

She stirred and struggled to push herself onto her knees, arms raised as her head lolled back to stare upward. Her eyes went distant and without looking, she pointed at the doorway.

"That's where you came through."

I froze. "What do you mean?"

"That's where the Titans sent you through. That's how you got to this realm." Roshanna's eyes drifted closed, and the emotionless plastic-like mask was gone, replaced by peace. Like a weight had been lifted off her shoulders. Small lines were visible in the corners of her eyes and the edges of her mouth, lines that revealed a lifetime of smiling and laughter. The more I looked at her the more she looked familiar, but I couldn't figure out why or where I may have seen her before.

Then she dropped back to the ground so suddenly, I could only stare as she hit the floor. I knelt, shaking her shoulder, but she didn't wake. "Roshanna?" I shook her harder. "Can you hear me? Roshanna!"

The unearthliness that made her so unsettling to look at began to peel back, like a layer of costume makeup was being washed away to reveal the person underneath. Freckles appeared, dappling her shoulders. The pulverized meat of her lips smoothed and her pristine porcelain skin pinked with the rosy hue of life.

"What's happening?" I murmured.

I looked around, uncertain what to do. I could load her over my shoulder and jump for the exit, but I didn't trust that the floor was stable enough to take that much weight all at once. I would probably end up dropping her and maybe injuring her. The way her body was changing, I wasn't sure if she could take that kind of fall.

But if we were in an underground chamber they had to have some way of getting down here that wasn't just dropping through a hole in the floor. Not to mention I'd never noticed them going in and out of this place when I was here so it couldn't have been something so obtrusive.

I got to my feet and skirted the room, running my fingers along the wall as I went. There was a space of blank wall in between each carved doorway, but as I passed a certain section, I noticed it felt... dead. Magick didn't run through this part the same way as the others, and it felt disconnected.

I didn't see a seam, but as I ran my hands along the wall my finger caught on some kind of switch concealed in the carved stone outline of the portal to my right. There was a click before some kind of illusion fell away and a door appeared.

A dark, narrow stairwell wound up and out of sight. I breathed a sigh of relief and went back to collect Roshanna, slinging her over my shoulder and heading up the stairs. At the top of the stairwell was a trapdoor, and I had to set her body down to put all my weight into opening it. Debris had crashed over top of it in the fire and it went flying as I gave one huge shove, the trap flinging open to reveal what had been my foster father's study.

Melted remnants of the absurd glass sculptures he'd kept in here were everywhere. I lifted the construct again, carefully picking my way toward the back door and outside.

The gardens were still there. While they were mostly untouched by the fire, they were badly in need of care. Everything was wild and overgrown, and I felt the tiniest bit of regret. These gardens were the only fond memory I had of this place, and they'd been left to rot.

I laid Roshanna down in the cushiest patch of grass I could find. Would Hades think I'd done something on purpose to harm her if I brought her back like this? Or would she be in danger now that whatever magick that had bound her was wearing off?

I'd just have to wait until she woke up.

I settled in.

CHAPTER NINE

Andrus

"What do we need to know?" I asked. The forest we were traveling through was beyond creepy and I half expected some of those creatures from Belsioch's prison realm to pop out at us.

Death stopped in his tracks and looked at me over his shoulder. "Don't get caught." Then he kept moving.

"That's it? That's all the sage advice we're going to get?"

Death shrugged. "I'm not sure what to tell you. I have no idea what you're walking into. I'm going to drop you down as close to his palace as I can get you. And then you're on your own. Don't let yourselves be seen. Stay away from any of his minions. I can't tell you if there are any traps, or where she might be. Because I don't know. Isn't strategy supposed to be your specialty?" he asked.

"Strategy, yes. But I don't have psychic abilities to just draw a map of this place from nothing. I need a little information to go off of." My anxiety was already through the roof having no knowledge to draw upon for this, and Death's flippant attitude was grating on my nerves. We'd be no good to Meg if we got caught. She was counting on us.

"I believe in you," he said, giving me a vapid smile before continuing on his merry way.

Gareth leaned in. "Don't worry about it overly much. Just focus on what you can do. You haven't failed us yet."

"Which means there's a first time for everything," I grumbled.

"This goes without saying, but I recommend getting back out as fast as you can," said Death.

"How are we getting out?" Remi asked.

I paused. *That* was a really good question. If Meg could draw up a portal, she would've left the second she had a chance.

"Hades can control everything in his realm. As long as he or one of the servants directly under his control has eyes on her, he can prevent her from leaving. But if you manage to get far enough away, or even if you just keep him distracted somehow, it should be enough. If the full portal isn't a possibility, have her do what she can to open one and I will help her from this side. Only if you have no other choice should you call me for help." Death gave me a look that threatened dire repercussions should we misuse that invitation and get him on the bad side of the lord of the Dark.

"Here we are," said Death. The spot that he stopped didn't look any different than anywhere else in the woods that we'd seen so far.

"Is there something different?" Gareth asked, just as clueless as I.

"It's thinner here," said Remi.

"Somebody is getting the hang of their new powers," said Death approvingly.

To me, Death resembled an old tutor of mine, a grizzled warrior that fought alongside my father as he seized his lands in Babylon. Ilan retired from the battlefield to become the meanest, most brutal, but most efficient teacher of swordsmanship that I ever had. I both feared and loved the man, and that's what made it all the more discomforting to see him before me now.

My father had killed him in a fit of rage after he'd taught me too well. I was able to best my father in a duel and Ilan had paid the price.

"That membrane between realms is easier to penetrate here," Death continued. "I can better control where you come out on the other side."

"Will he notice our arrival if we're around the edge of his territory?" I asked.

"My hope is that even if he does notice, he won't recognize your signatures. Meg stands out. The minute she opened that portal to send Arthur's soul back, he would've recognized the significance. But you? Fools come and go occasionally, and he pays them no mind. You're just curious thrill seekers who are soon to find out they're getting more than they bargained for. Not worth his time."

Not exactly the sterling motivation I was hoping for, but it was better than nothing. I took a deep breath and prepared myself, noticing my brothers do the same. It would be just the three of us in the underworld alone, looking for our mate in a place we were so unfamiliar with that I couldn't even wrap my head around what we were about to walk into. Orchestrating the siege of a mountaintop fortress would've been a preferable chore to the one we were facing.

"See you soon," said Gareth, giving Death a brisk nod.

"Counting on it," he replied.

And then the world around us shifted, a mere blink of an eye finding us in a strange new landscape. A walled city rose before us, several tiers partitioned off by sections of walls and gates, leading up to a massive palace at the crest of the slope. The palace itself was a blinding white, blistering as it reflected the artificial sunlight breaking in overhead.

The city was set in perfect weather, but the area we were standing in now was shaded in gloom and mist. "I've heard stories, but I've never seen it with my own eyes," said Gareth.

"Did Meg ever talk to either of you about it?" Remi asked.

I shook my head. "No. The time she spent here was always better avoided in her mind. Farah speaking of the Gieses was the first time I'd heard anything about the family that raised her." Anger flared in my chest at the thought. Those monsters had done irreparable damage, making her perfectly susceptible to Belsioch's lies about the Titans. I couldn't blame her for the hatred she'd held for Kronos and the rest of her kin for so long.

The land surrounding the outermost wall of the city, everywhere the artificial sunlight touched, was lush and green. The second that pool of light gave away to the shadow, it was barren wasteland all around. Nothing but scrub and the hardiest of plants even tried to withstand it.

Far, far in the distance, I could see mountains and the golden shimmer of wheat. But immediately around the city was a dead zone. No pun intended.

The area we were walking in was rough underfoot until we reached the dividing line between sun and shade. Then, a palisade opened before us, made of pristine, crushed white rock that glittered with mica. The bottom gate stood open, and there were no guards I could see.

"Should we be worried?" asked Remi, concern evident as his stone skin drew around him. He didn't bother to hide his wings, not here. "They just leave the gate open to visitors?"

I shrugged, but as we moved through the gate, I saw the hustle and bustle, a frantic energy that had people moving ahead with single-mindedness that made them oblivious to everything else.

I noted several servants wearing livery indicative of a noble house surrounded by lesser servants, carrying all sorts of goods as they made their way back up the tiers of the city to their households. Two more levels up we saw much the same, except here people were prepping their grounds, sweeping, trimming, tidying up. Elaborate topiaries were being reshaped. A show was being put on.

"There's a party happening, I'd bet my life on it," I said. The gods knew I'd been witness to enough of these events, put on only to stroke egos and show off elaborate wealth.

"One of Hades's?" Gareth asked.

I cast my gaze along the road, following it upward to the palace. Along the entire way were signs that every household and street was getting a deep clean, and I could just see servants crawling around the palace, tiny black dots in the distance. "That's a safe assumption."

"This could be great for us, right?" Remi asked. "We can sneak in right under their noses. They won't even know we're there in all the commotion."

"That's an option," I said, already keeping an eye out for things to steal, clothing to wear. "I don't know if we should risk attending as guests, but I'm sure there will be plenty of staff on site." I considered. "It would allow us to move freely around the party and get close to her if we see her."

"You think he'd take the risk of letting her mingle at the party?" Gareth asked, frowning.

I nodded. "Why would he have any reason to fear? Even if she says that she's being kept here against her will, nobody would dare go against Hades himself. In his own house, no less."

A low growl issued from Gareth and Remi both as they considered the implications, blatant wrongdoings flaunted in public places that were overlooked as long as the person committing them was powerful enough.

I hadn't expected this many issues from my past to come calling, and yet here I was. Fighting long-dormant demons that weren't as buried as I thought.

We kept climbing, each tier falling away quickly as we made our way unimpeded toward the palace.

"Wait," said Gareth, holding up his hand. He'd caught a scent.

"Is it her?" I asked. My Nosmortem blood did allow me superior senses, but they still weren't nearly as keen as Gareth's.

He smiled, his relief evident as his shoulders relaxed just a millimeter farther away from his ears. "Yes. And there's no hint of fear. There is one other scent that accompanies hers, but I can't make heads or tails of it."

I nodded. "Can you follow without us being too obvious?"

Gareth glanced around. "Pretty sure."

The crowds weren't nearly as compacted up here, but there was still plenty of activity to hide within. He led us toward the burned-out husk of a building.

"They just leave a ruin like this in the uppermost tier of the city?" Remi asked.

"This must be the Giese's residence," I said. The few pieces of information that Meg shared about her time here measured out.

We picked our way inside. There wasn't much to see, but even I was picking up Meg's scent here. It couldn't have been more than a few hours since she'd been through, and my heart lifted. All I wanted was to grab her up in my arms again.

"Come check this out." Remi's call came from another room, and I followed.

I found him and Gareth standing over a hole in the floor. "What'd you find?"

"Not sure. There's a steady thrum of magick, and she was definitely down there."

"I'll check it out," said Remi, jumping down before we could say anything otherwise. I heard his wings engage briefly to slow his descent and a small flicker of light appeared in the gloom.

"It's a portal room," he said, voice echoing in a strangely distorted manner.

"Can you tell where they lead?" I asked.

"No. It doesn't seem like any of them have been used recently, either." There was a rush of wind and Remi appeared again, shooting out of the whole with his wings tucked in.

Gareth jerked his head to the side for us to follow. "Her scent leads back this way."

We walked around the back of the house, coming out into a small garden. It must've been quite a sight back in its day.

"They spent a while right here," he said, motioning to a spot of crushed grass. "Before moving on that way." He pointed over a garden wall which led back to the main street. "They must've gone back to the palace."

The three of us stared up the high walls. The house of Hades didn't seem overly intimidating from the outside, but what better way to put people at ease? I could only imagine what difficulties we would face inside, but it was worth every bit of the risk.

"We're coming, Meg," I murmured.

CHAPTER TEN

Meg

About ten minutes later, Roshanna began to stir, groaning as she sat up.

"Did something happen?" she asked.

"You passed out. Right after you said something about that portal room being used to bring me through as a baby."

She looked around at me, dazed. "I said that?"

I nodded. "You don't remember?" I cocked my head. "Or you weren't supposed to say anything?"

Roshanna attempted to stand, and I helped her up. I released her arm and went to step away, but she clasped my hands in her own. "You can't tell Master Hades that I said anything. You shouldn't even tell him we've been speaking as much as we have."

"Why?" I asked. "How much does he know about the Gieses? Their deal with the Titans?"

She hesitated, not wanting to say anything further.

"I'm not going to tell him that we spoke. In fact, if you want help getting out of here—"

"No," she said quickly, her hands clamping down harder on mine before she realized what she was doing and eased up. "I can't leave." Roshanna released my hands entirely and took a deliberate step back. "But I appreciate the offer."

"Can you just tell me what's going on? What's it going to hurt?" I asked.

"It's not my place. And I can't even be sure that I know the truth."

"I'll take whatever you've got."

After quiet deliberation, she nodded. "Let's walk and talk."

We fell into step as we headed back toward the palace. "This is all based on what I've heard over the years. All of this happened before I was created. The Gieses we're always angling for a position above the power they'd already been afforded. It was a not-so-subtle secret that if they could've knocked Hades off his throne and taken it for themselves, they would have."

"He allowed them to stay here, knowing that?"

Roshanna snorted softly. "He wasn't concerned. That whole family was rather delusional. And when you showed up, he just thought it added to the entertainment. The thought that they would be able to ride the coattails of a *chosen one*..." She rolled her eyes, her distaste dripping around the words.

She continued to talk, that hollow voice giving away to a more human one. The echo was gone, and her mouth matched the words as she spoke them.

That raised a question that I had to interrupt her to ask. "What happened to you? You don't seem like you're Hades's puppet anymore. Your body changed and it doesn't sound like somebody else is speaking through you."

She shook her head. "I do feel a lot more... myself, than I have in a long time. So much changed about a year ago." Her brows knit. "Practically the entire household staff was moved or let go. And mistress Persephone hasn't been seen for some time."

"Is she missing?" Considering what happened last time she went off the grid, I didn't like the implications.

"No. He is still receiving communication from her."

Just the way that Roshanna said it, told me she didn't believe it. Then my strange encounter in the dungeons came to mind. Could that have been her?

"You mentioned that Hades created you. But in the portal room, you said that you were brought through there." I left the question open-ended, not sure what, if anything, I was implying.

She stopped in her tracks, confused. "That doesn't make any sense."

I tried asking a couple more questions, but let the matter drop when I wasn't getting anywhere.

"Do you know where Hades is supposed to be today? Will he be busy with party prep? Or does somebody else handle that for him?" I asked. If I was going back to the dungeons to explore, I didn't want a repeat close encounter like the one the other night.

She nodded. "He likes to keep an eye on things. Make sure everything is to his taste. Another thing that changed about him. He used to hate these ordeals."

"And this will keep him busy all day?" I asked.

"Assuredly," she agreed. "Why?"

I shook my head. "No reason. Just trying to plan the rest of my day."

There was suspicion in her gaze, but it was accompanied by a mischievous approval. "Well, as soon as we get back to the palace, I'll have plenty of other things to keep me occupied. So I guess you'll be on your own. Try not to get into too much trouble."

"Of course not," I said.

"I will be back to check on you a few hours before the party starts, however. Just so you're aware."

We had reentered the palace grounds, the preparations for the party going full-tilt as people skittered about, trying to make everything perfect.

"This is where I'll leave you then," said Roshanna, bowing slightly at the waist and giving me a wink.

Before she could walk off, I stopped her. "Will anyone notice?" I asked. "You do look a little different."

She brushed me off. "Most people around here don't notice anyone on the service staff. And my coworkers wouldn't say anything." She grinned. "I'll be fine."

We parted ways, and I prepared to infiltrate a dungeon.

I cursed, tripping on an uneven stair and wondering how the hell I'd made it down here sleepwalking. That familiar cold, damp, biting air surrounded me as I found myself in the chamber that split off into three passageways. I'd been traveling down the middle one, right? That's where I heard the cries coming from last time? It was still a blur.

For the first time since I'd woken up down here with no memory of the trip, I wondered if it had all been some strange dream.

Then I heard the cries. The same sniffling, fearful whimpers. Nothing in my gut was telling me this was a trap, and the fear I heard in the woman's voice had been genuine when I overheard her being questioned by Hades. I pulled my stone skin around myself, also reaching for Felix's illusion magic and calling forth my claws and fangs. Even though my mates weren't with me, they were still enabling me to keep myself safe. I wondered what they were doing? Had they made it back from Bel's prison realm?

Would Arthur's soul be okay? The second I had a chance, I would escape. It already seemed like Roshanna was on my side. If I got far enough away from this place, potentially with her help, I could summon another portal and be gone.

But I needed to focus. I was at the point I had turned around last time, and I took a deep breath. Whatever I was about to find wouldn't be pleasant. But it would hopefully provide plenty of answers, and maybe allow me to get a foot up on whatever he was planning.

I still didn't believe that he wanted to hasten the Ætherim's end. Death had mentioned that Hades was going a little soft in the mind, so there was no telling what his ultimate plans were, but...

I could see a slight change of light up ahead, a flickering aspect. The slow curve of the hallway gave way to the view of the door, and I crept close to it, keeping as silent as possible. It reminded me a lot of the door to Remi's prison cell, heavy iron, just a small grate to peek through at the top, but underneath it, instead of just solid darkness, light diffused into the hallway from the small crack at the bottom.

I had to stand on tiptoe to see through the window, and I waited for my eyes to adjust, the firelight casting heavy shadows and messing with my head. The outline of a woman lying prone on the floor on some kind of makeshift cot near the fire came into focus. Her shoulders shook as she cried, attempting to muffle her sound by burying her face in her arms.

There was a certain creep factor, I realized, as I stood there watching this woman. Should I say something? What if she freaked out and drew attention? I wasn't sure if we were alone down here, not entirely.

My gaze must've drawn her attention regardless. She stirred, pushing up onto an elbow and staring at the door. "Is someone there?" she asked.

The minute I got a good look at her face, I gasped. "Lady Persephone?" She looked exhausted and terrified, and I'd only ever seen her in passing, but I knew it was her.

"Who are you?" she asked, her voice sharp.

"I'm here to help," I said, wanting to put her at ease but not sure how. My name wouldn't mean anything to her. Telling her what I was wouldn't help the situation either. "Did your husband trap you in here?"

"No," she said, looking at something out of my range of view. "That thing wearing my husband's face is not Hades."

Shit. That complicates things.

I examined the latch on the door, checking the surrounding area for a key. She must've guessed what I was doing. "He keeps the key on himself at all times."

"That's fine," I said. There were plenty of ways around that. I held my hand to the lock, constructing a small bubble of time around it before turning the clock forward. It rusted underneath my fingers until it disintegrated into dust and I could easily pull the door open.

Persephone watched me enter, shock plain on her face. "Who are you?" she asked again, but the question held a deeper resonance this time.

"Megiste," I said. "You probably remember hearing about me—"

"The construct of the Titans?"

I dipped my head in acknowledgment. "Yes."

"What are you doing here?" she asked. "You escaped the Gieses. You should be well along your quest by now."

"I had to take a slight detour. Recover one of our own."

Now that I was inside the cell, I got a much better look at the other occupant. Hades was lying, seemingly unconscious, on a pallet. He'd been tucked in and it looked like he was being cared for attentively.

"He won't wake," she said, noticing my gaze. "He's been like that ever since that imposter took over."

"So who is it? The person posing as Hades?" I asked.

"I don't know a name. All I know is that he's some kind of chaos demon."

My heart thudded painfully. "You don't say."

"I take it you've had run-in with these creatures before?"

"Legion," I said, nodding. "What does this one want?"

Persephone sniffed. "The vessel that gives Hades lordship over the underworld use to be contained where all the rivers converge, but he moved it. It was too vulnerable. The demon wants it, but I won't tell him where it is. And his interrogation of my husband didn't go as planned. Hades put himself in this state, so the demon couldn't read his mind."

"How long have you been down here?" I asked.

She shook her head. "I'm not sure. This creature showed up wearing the face of another, becoming a trusted advisor of my husband. Then, by the time we realized there was something off about him, he'd already integrated himself too far into our lives. He made his move, imprisoned us down here and took my husband's place. Until he finds that vessel, he can't kill us." Her voice broke. "But I don't know how much longer it will be. As long as he wears that face, nobody will stand in his way on his search, and he can take all the time he needs."

"Let's get you out of here, to somewhere safe," I said.

"No," she said. "The minute he realizes we're gone, there's no telling what he'll do."

"What if we find a way to wake him?" I asked, inclining my head toward Hades. "If he has backup, will he be able to push the demon out?"

Persephone gazed at her husband sadly. "I don't know. That thing is powerful. It was only out of desperation that he put himself in that state." Tears welled in her eyes. "I don't even know if he *can* wake up."

I reached out and gently touched her shoulder. "I have a knack for finding creative solutions to things. We'll figure this out."

She nodded, keeping her reservation close. There was no way she was going to get her hopes up at the word of some stranger she'd only heard about in rumor.

"I'll put an illusion on the door, so it looks like the lock is still there. If things go sideways, at least it will give you a way to escape."

Persephone offered me a small smile. "I appreciate the sentiment."

After closing the door behind me and weaving a small illusion, hoping the demon wouldn't have any reason to come down here before the party and test out the imaginary lock, I made my way back upstairs, mind spinning as it tried to work out a plan.

Why did every side quest and detour turn into something life or death? I had thought it was just bad luck, but now I wasn't so sure. I was starting to think of it along the same lines as to why the Six always ended up in places of upheaval. They were drawn to where people needed the most help, where they could do the most good.

What if the Fates were directing us in this as well? That what seemed like disasters and mistakes were all supposed to happen exactly as they had? Destiny in action?

Head swimming with the possibilities, I closed the door at the top of the stairs behind me and made to sneak back through the kitchens, hoping the staff was still at a minimum so the illusion I wrapped around myself wouldn't be tested by running into someone.

Then I turned a corner, and all my worries vanished in an instant.

Chapter Eleven

Gareth

Her scent still lingered on the air. We were close. Andrus had sneaked us into the back of the palace, and liberated a few extra uniforms from the laundry. So far, we were easily passing as servants as we moved through the lower floors.

We had just turned a corner after passing through the kitchens when I halted in my tracks. Her scent was so strong here, it was like she was standing right in front of us.

And then her illusion dropped, and Meg was there, tears in her eyes and a smile on her face. She threw herself at us and my arms instinctively wrapped around her as I buried my face in her neck, and Remi and Andrus surrounded her on either side.

"How did you find me so fast? How did you get here? Did Arthur make it back into his body?" she asked, not pausing for an answer in between her rapid-fire questioning.

They were only a couple of servants in the hall, and they barely even gave us the time of day, too busy going about their tasks. I moved Meg along until we found a small open room and

I pulled her in, kissing her before giving her space to greet the others. Remi swept her up in a crushing hug before setting her down, his kiss light and tender.

Andrus wrapped her in his arms, touching his forehead to hers and whispering something I couldn't quite hear, but the smile on her face said enough. She turned in his arms to speak to us, but he didn't let her go, resting his chin on the top of her head.

"We need to go," I said. "Everyone's distracted, it will be simple to sneak out the back. Once we get outside the city—"

"We can't leave. Not yet."

The three of us stared at her in open-mouthed shock. "Of course we can," I said. "Once we get away from Hades's influence—"

The cross look on her face made me pause. "But you knew that already."

"I mean, there's something else we need to do before we can leave."

Meg looked around, conscious of prying ears and eyes. "Follow me," she said, leading us upstairs and to the guest room Hades had put her in. As soon as the heavy door was shut, she explained everything that had happened since she had arrived. Andrus resumed his place behind her, and I had to tamp down my jealousy at the small smile of contented comfort that it brought her. She was happy, and she felt safe. That's all that mattered, no matter how much my wolf argued with the notion.

"Another chaos demon?" said Remi, shaking his head. "Why do we keep running across these creatures?"

Meg was just as baffled as us but there was something in her eyes as she spoke. "Could it be fate? Are the Fates orchestrating all of this? Maybe there's something involving these chaos demons that we need to figure out. Something that's part of the plan. Kronos didn't have a whole lot of time to explain it to me, maybe he left that out."

"Or maybe they're working with Belsioch." Andrus's eyes widened. "You don't know. We spoke with Risha."

Meg spun to look at him. "When?"

Andrus gave her the abbreviated version of our own experiences, her face becoming more crestfallen with each new blow he dealt. "So he's back up to full power again? And he's merged with Legion?" She scrubbed both hands over her face. "And Risha has found some kind of working relationship with the Hounds..." She laughed. "That's a sentence I never thought I would say." She looked at me. "But otherwise Risha is okay?"

"I'd say she's more than alright," I said, shaking my head at the entire enterprise. "She's taken charge of whatever operation Belsioch was running. She's also confident that she trapped him in medieval France, so with any luck, he won't be able to bother us here."

"Won't he just be able to slip into the Strangefells or the underworld even? Slip back into our time through the realms? Or does whatever time he's stuck in apply to any realm he might enter?" Remi asked.

Time was ready and waiting with an answer for me to give. "No. Theoretically, it might be possible. It depends on how he's traveling through time. Since he doesn't have a natural ability with it, chances are good that if he tries to slip into another realm, the dissonance would be too great. It would shred him to pieces. He'll have to find somebody else that can manipulate time in order to escape."

"And there aren't a whole lot of those available," said Meg, nodding her agreement to my explanation. "With any luck, we'll be safe for a little longer yet. But if anyone's going to figure it out…"

"What can we do against the chaos demon here? The Hounds themselves had trouble with Legion. We aren't even sure which one this is," said Remi.

"I'm going to try to wake Hades up. He put himself in some kind of trance, receded within his own mind to try to hide what he knew."

"How are you going to get through to him?" Andrus asked.

She shook her head. "Not sure yet. I think I'm going to have to phone a friend, get some advice."

She stiffened and her eyes became frantic as she looked us over, as if she expected us to fade away in front of her. "Shit. It's not safe for you to be here."

"It's alright," Remi soothed. "Our connection to you offers us some protection. I can feel it even stronger now that we're next to you."

Her face softened as she looked at him, that fear abating. I moved to her and caressed her cheek, and she leaned her face into my palm.

"I love you," she said. "All of you. I'm glad you came."

There was a knock at the door, and we all froze.

"Meg?" called a voice at the same time I caught the scent of the person at the door. They'd been with Meg in the ruins of her old house.

She crossed to the door and motioned us to the side, out of line of sight of the doorway. Once we had taken our positions, she pulled the door open, greeting the woman on the other side. "Is it time already?" she asked.

"Almost. Master Hades wanted me to check in. He'll be sending up your costume shortly, but if there's anything else you need in the meantime." The voice was hollow and sounded oddly dissonant. Meg stiffened and I readied myself for an attack, but it wasn't fear. She was surprised and off-put by something.

"I'm fine. Thank you."

There was no reply, but Meg smiled awkwardly before closing the door.

"What's wrong?" I asked.

She rolled her shoulders, brow furrowed. "That was a construct of Hades's, Roshanna. She's been accompanying me around the city. Earlier today, it seemed like she was changing, becoming more human, but now—" She lifted her hand to her mouth and started chewing on her thumbnail. "It's like she's back to the way she was before. Hades regained complete control over her."

There was more noise in the hall outside carrying up from the floor below. Guests must be arriving.

"We should head back down and blend in. When she comes back, I'm sure there'll be servants with her to help you change," said Andrus.

"Yeah," she said, her mind still lost in thought. She blinked and focused on us. "Are you going to be alright?"

"So far there haven't been any problems," I assured her. "Nobody's been the wiser to the three new servants."

"After the party begins, we'll meet up where I ran into you," she said. "Then we can head down to the dungeons and try to figure out how to help Persephone."

"Alright," I said, reluctant to leave her. Everything in me wanted to grab her and run, consequences be damned. This wasn't our fight. They were things of much greater importance that we needed to focus on, and if something happened to any of us… I swallowed the words. There was no way any of us could convince Meg to leave and turn her back on people she had already vowed to help.

"Be safe," she said, giving each of us a kiss before we headed out the door.

We hurried along the passageways, reaching the main floor without incident or run-ins with any other staff. Activity on this floor was at a fever pitch. Food was being set out on great banquet tables, the final touches were being put on the decorations, and guests were trickling in.

"You three," barked a voice.

I looked around to find a small man with watery eyes and sallow skin staring up at me and my companions. "Did Gorman send you down here?"

I have a lot of good qualities, but thinking fast while under interrogation is not one of them. Luckily, Andrus stepped up to the plate.

"No. We're here in advance of the Lomands," he said, naming one of the few underworld noble families that I'd heard of.

The little man blustered. "In advance. This is preposterous. They don't trust us to get everything in order for their arrival?"

Andrus put his hand on the man's shoulder. "It's nothing to do with you or your household. This is all for us," he said, motioning at myself and Remi. "We're trying to make an effort to prove our worth to the family. Move up in the world, you know? If we make sure that they are perfectly positioned at this event, we can see some real upward mobility."

The man's frown deepened as he listened to this explanation, but he didn't immediately call our bluff. "Your goal may be sympathetic," he said, voice turning chill, "but I don't want you around the next time I come through here. We've got everything well under control."

"Understood," said Andrus, giving the man a sharp nod. "Can't blame us for trying though."

The man looked like he very much could blame us for that, but he had much more important things to deal with and hurried off.

"Quick thinking, friend," said Remi, holding back a chuckle.

"Let's do what he requested, and make ourselves scarce," I said, not wanting to linger and push our luck. If one more person took notice of us, I was calling this scheme off and we would just hide until it was time to act. I had plenty of confidence in Andrus's abilities to get us out of tight spots, but I wasn't taking unnecessary risks.

Especially now we knew we were dealing with a chaos demon.

Chapter Twelve

Meg

Roshanna returned with an entire group of stylists along with the dress the tailor had made for me. It was stunning. Long, black satin flowed to the ground with a train that looked like feathers edged in gold. The bodice was a corset with a soft velvet exterior and gold piping studded with gems.

I was ushered into a changing area where the team went to work. The procedure wasn't unknown to me, but even when the Gieses forced me to dress up to show me off, at least the servants and I had bonded over our mutual hatred of them.

These women had none of that. They were cold and distant, ignoring every attempt I made at conversation. I wasn't sure if that should make me more nervous—maybe this was just how they were—but it certainly didn't help.

When the transformation was complete, they stood me in front of a floor-length mirror and I couldn't help but gasp. The gown was flawless, my hair had been done up in some elaborate style that was all curls and braids, and when they fitted the mask over my face, I briefly lost that sense of who I was.

"Master Hades will be pleased," said Roshanna.

"Doesn't he already know," I asked, knowing full-well that he was staring out of her eyes.

She only smiled that grotesque, twisted smile, and cocked her head to the side. "The party begins in thirty minutes. Master Hades expects to see you at the top of the stairs."

I nodded, and the entire team swept out of the room. A relieved breath gushed out of my lungs as soon as I was alone again, but I regretted it. The corset was so tight, drawing breath wasn't a fun time.

Before I had to make my appearance, I put my mind to better use than worrying. I needed to figure out a way to wake the real Hades out of his trance.

After my impromptu visit, and potential massive fuck up, I hadn't called out to the Titans since. But once we were down in those dungeons, we wouldn't have any time to waste. I needed to figure this out now.

My attempt at taking a seat was foiled by my complete inability to breathe, so I settled for leaning against the wall.

Despite my rattling nerves, I slipped into a light trance easily enough, drifting into that gray place between realms.

Kronos, I called. And then I waited.

Megiste. The answer came so suddenly, the deep voice echoing in my mind, that I almost startled out of my trance.

Hades and Persephone are in trouble. He's in a trance, they're being held by a chaos demon. I need to wake him up, but I'm not sure what to do.

A rumbling boom I took as a thoughtful hum, rippled through my brain, but I received no answer. *I know this may not seem like something I should focus on right now, but I can't just leave them like this. This is a chaos demon we're talking about. Bel has merged with Legion. I don't think it's a coincidence that I've run across another one.*

Belsioch merged *with a chaos demon?* Kronos asked, alarm clear in his voice.

Yes. That's the word I received, anyway. I haven't seen evidence of it myself, but the person that told us about it would have no reason to lie.

That is very grim news indeed, he said.

Persephone said the demon here is looking for the vessel that ties Hades to the underworld. I'm not sure exactly what his plans are for it, but I don't think anybody would assume they were good.

A sigh, very much like a strong wind rattling dry leaves, came from Kronos. *You are right. I don't know why the chaos demons are making themselves such a nuisance, now of all times, but ignoring it now could mean dire consequences later, when we can afford the distraction even less. And if Belsioch is connected to them how you surmise...*

There was a long pause. *I'm still working on finding a way around... the mistake I made,* I said, knowing that that word wasn't quite strong enough for the conundrum I'd caused.

I would expect nothing less, he said, a proud but sad note in his voice. He didn't believe I'd be able to find a way around it. I guess I'd just have to prove him wrong.

Selene has a solution to your problem. Call upon her when you are ready, and she'll guide you through it, he said.

Thank you, I said, feeling the connection sever.

Selene, Titan of the moon, of hidden and secret things.

There was a lighter knock at the door, and I knew just from the sound of it that it wasn't Roshanna. "It's time," a voice called through.

"Coming," I called back, heading for the door.

Hades was waiting at the top of the stairs, just like Roshanna had said he would be. It all made sense. There was a pervading wrongness that I couldn't place before, but I'd chalked it up to Death's warnings. You never expect a monster to be wearing somebody else's face so convincingly. Even though I've seen plenty of glamours and illusions, this was something else.

The man that wasn't Hades crooked his elbow and offered his arm and I placed my hand lightly on it.

"You look lovely, the tailor did well," he purred.

"Thank you, Lord Hades," I said.

"Are you ready for your grand entrance?" he asked.

"This is your party, my lord, I'm just here at your request," I replied, giving him an easy smile and trying to still the rapid thud of my heartbeat.

We started down the stairs, the carpet muffling our footsteps, mine in black stilettos, his in fine Italian-leather dress shoes. I could hear the susurrus of many voices down below, and as the long stairway dipped beneath the floor above it, I finally got a glimpse of the entire ground floor.

It was packed with people, all of them in equally fine masquerade gowns, suits, and masks. And every face was directed at us. The murmurs became conspiratorial whispers as they realized who I was. It may have been fifty years since Bel had murdered my foster family, burned the house down, and "rescued" me, but people this long-lived don't forget things like that. To them I'm sure the memories were still crisp, like it only happened yesterday.

"Ladies and gentlemen," said Hades, stopping us two steps from the bottom stair. I scanned the crowd, looking for familiar faces among the servants, but my mates were nowhere to be found. Hopefully they were still staying under the radar.

"Thank you all for coming," he continued. "I'm sure you've realized by now who our special guest is for this evening."

More whispers and a few nods.

"She's been living quite the exciting life outside of our borders. I'm sure she'll be more than happy to regale all who ask with the stories."

Or not. Most definitely not.

"But for now, let's just give her a proper welcome home."

Polite clapping rose up from the crowd, accompanied by dead-eyed stares. Exactly the kind of welcome home I would've expected.

"Welcome all," said Hades, holding his arms out wide. "My home is your own for this evening. Let the festivities begin!"

A small string quartet in the corner began to play, a jaunty medieval tune I'm sure was all the rage during the childhoods of most people here.

"I will leave you to catch up with your old neighbors. I'm sure you'll have lots to talk about," said Hades.

With the masks on, I couldn't distinguish who was who. There were no discernible features allowing me to put names to the concealed faces. The Gieses had many enemies, and they'd flaunted me in front of them as often as they could just to make a statement about their alliances with the Titans. Nobody here could be counted on as a "friend."

My skin crawled as I realized how much danger I was truly in. Hades, or the chaos demon inside him, was a factor that I was prepared for. But now, standing in front of all these snakes, who would gladly stab me in the back, or the front, or between the eyes, a new thread of fear wrapped around me.

"Did you have your tailor make this dress out of bullet-, and stab-proof material?" I asked through a fake smile.

He chuckled. "Nobody will bring any harm to you within these walls. They wouldn't dare. Please, enjoy yourself. You have nothing to fear." Hades leaned in close and spoke into my ear. "There's even a surprise guest I'm sure you'll be excited to meet."

He straightened and walked off without another word, disappearing into the crowd and leaving me alone in a den of vipers on tenuous leashes.

CHAPTER THIRTEEN

Meg

Lady Carolena was the first to approach me, her razor-sharp teeth and snide tone the only reason I recognized her. She'd been a regular visitor to the Gieses and used to advise on various ways to punish me for my impropriety.

"So nice to see you back," she said, dragging a handheld fan from somewhere on her person, flicking it open and fanning her face.

"It's not permanent," I said, narrowing my eyes.

"I can see you're heartbroken over your family's demise." Her simpering smile made me want to wipe it off her face.

"They weren't my family. And no, I'm not heartbroken." I grinned, a dark mimic of her own. "Not that you were too torn up either. Nobody was. Their bodies are still in that burned-out wreck. I should've added one of their skulls to my costume."

She scoffed, disgusted, snapping her fan shut. "You never did understand anything they did for you."

I raised a single eyebrow and stared her down. "Correct. And I don't want to."

Carolena's lip curled in a sneer and she walked away, her sycophant husband trailing behind her. He didn't even spare me a sideways glance.

I continued moving through the room, making my way toward our intended rendezvous point. There were plenty of poisonous glares and shows of teeth, but nobody else approached me until I made it into the next room, a parlor by all appearances. The crush of people was a bit thinner in here, most lounging around on low furniture.

"Megiste," said a deep voice. A man approached from my left. He didn't have any of the giveaways that Carolena did.

I bowed my head. "You know me, but I'm afraid I can't figure out who you are. Apologies." Slipping back into the courtly mannerisms that were beaten into me when I was young was far easier than I thought it would be.

"Piotr. Romanov," he added, when the first name didn't ring any bells. It still took me a minute to place him. The Romanovs, while a formidable family, were never directly at war with the Gieses. Most of the time there was an amiable working relationship between the two families. Piotr was their youngest son, or at least he had been. It seemed like there was always a new addition to that family every time I turned around. Great for ensuring the family business would always stay in the family, but terrible when it came to infighting.

"Piotr, nice to see you again," I said. It wasn't strictly a lie. From what I remember, he was always annoying and spoiled, but not as terrible as some of his other siblings.

"You're still a great liar," he said, grinning. "But I don't blame you."

"How is your family?"

He made a face and waved his hand. "They're fine." Through his tiger mask, I could see him roll his eyes. "Still the same backstabbing cutthroats as always. I'm sure my mother—rest her soul—would be the first to thank you for bringing about the demise of the Gieses. It doubled our bottom line."

"Your mother died?" I asked. Strange to leave that out.

"No. She's the same old wretch she's always been. I just say that as a mantra. Wishful thinking I guess."

My eyes widened and I forced a smile to my face. "Well, it's been nice catching up, but I need to keep making the rounds."

"Of course. After you make your first circuit, perhaps you'll come back and share some of your adventures." His eyes glittered.

"I'd love to," I assured him, giving him another bow before moving on.

I was just turning the corner and closing in on our meeting place when I ran into someone turning the corner from the other side. I was only about chest height on this guy—not saying much given how short I am—but he was also burly and wide. His mask covered his entire face except for his eyes, a deep brown color that was sparkling with some kind of recognition.

"Apologies," he purred. Goosebumps broke out on my skin, and I wanted to bolt. What he said had been so benign, but the way he said it... he pitched his voice awkwardly, adding a bit of a warble, like he was trying to alter it. Why would he feel the need to do that?

"Not at all," I said, skirting around him and walking quickly away, trying not to look back over my shoulder. I was so focused on escape that I almost walked right past my mates.

"Meg," Andrus whispered.

Doubling back, I ducked into the room just off the kitchen that they were using to store the excess party supplies which were stacked everywhere.

"Wow," said Andrus, getting the full view of me. "You look amazing."

Silent nods of agreement from Gareth and Remi as they looked at me with their intense gazes and soft smiles made me forget what we were doing for a moment.

"This ol' thing?" I joked, pulling the ibis mask off my face. A servant bustled past on their way to the kitchens and I jumped, but they didn't even notice us.

"Any problems?" Remi asked. "You seem worried."

I shook my head. "Just a lot of ghosts from my past and a creepy guest. This house is filled with enemies at the moment. Not to freak anybody out," I added lamely.

"That was a given," Gareth assured me. "Let's go. We've already lingered for longer than I would like."

"Also a given," Andrus teased.

The door to the dungeon was standing open just a crack as we approached. It could've been completely innocuous, but my nerves became just that little bit more frazzled.

"This is our best chance. We have to go now," said Gareth, urging me forward.

He was right, but I still had to fight against my instinct to take that step through the doorway. We made our way down and I headed directly for Persephone's cell, breathing a sigh of relief to find it the same as I left it.

"Persephone?" I called. "I brought some help."

Moving cautiously inside, I peered through the dim light. The fire had died down to embers and a chill was stealing its way back in.

"Over here," she said. She was kneeling beside Hades, holding his hands and looking at my mates curiously. "Who are they?"

"Gareth, Andrus, and Remi," I replied, giving them each an introduction. "They're my mates. You can trust them."

"They are members of the Titans' inner circle?" she asked.

"Yes," said Andrus. "We will do everything we can to help."

I joined Persephone kneeling at Hades's side. His skin had been washed and perfumed.

She seemed to know what I was thinking. "No matter what the legends say, I do love my husband. And he loves me."

Persephone said it with a soft conviction. She wasn't trying to convince me, she was just letting me know.

"I'm not sure how this is going to work. Before the party, I reached out to Kronos, hoping he would have an idea of what to do. He told me to call on Selene and she'd guide me through it."

"And you're confident? That you can trust them? My husband was no enemy of theirs, but all I can recall about the Titans themselves is that their general opinion of the Ætherim as a whole is... poor."

"Their motivations are rooted in the desire for people's well-being. It's been a learning experience for me as well."

She nodded and released her husband's hands, moving away from his body. Not an hour ago, I was walking down the stairs with his double. It was surreal.

"Selene," I said, lulling myself into a light trance. "Please come. Help me wake him."

What started as another consciousness poking around at the edge of my mind soon became a presence. Selene burst forward, her entire being filling my mind, and I reached out blindly for my mates to steady me.

The three of them surrounded me, imbuing me with their calm.

I raised my hand to Hades's forehead and rested it on his cold skin. Selene surged forward, acting through me, sifting through his mind on a deep dive. She pushed his barriers aside with great care, working her way past the blockade he'd erected to keep the chaos demon out.

There. It was just a flicker of light, a subtle energy, but Selene dove for it. I could feel the strain it was causing her to be so careful when it was already a monumental effort to be here in the first place.

In my mind's eye came an image of Hades, sleeping in his self-induced coma. He had created a world within his own mind, a bubble to hide within. Selene reached for him, calling for him to wake, appealing directly to the man buried so deeply inside himself that nobody else would have been able to reach him. But this was all child's play to a Titan who ruled over the hidden.

She called for him again, an action I felt rather than heard, and this time there was a response. Hades stirred, just a small twitch. Another call, and his eyes fluttered before creeping open.

"It's safe," I said out loud, the words harsh in my ears after such intense concentration.

Persephone appeared in my peripheral, taking his hands again. "We need you back, love. Please. We need to fight back."

A smile crept across his face as he recognized her voice. The self buried within him leaped forward and Hades's corpse-still body came to life again.

Selene disappeared the second his eyes opened into the real world and I fell back into the waiting arms of my mates, head spinning.

Persephone was leaning over Hades, her forehead against his as she whispered to him. The four of us gave them some space.

"That was intense," Andrus said. "I could feel Selene's power moving through you."

Remi nodded. "It was almost like being back in their presence again."

Gareth dabbed at my sweaty face with his sleeve. "Are you alright?"

"Yeah." I nodded, still catching my breath. "Channeling a Titan is like sticking your finger in an electrical outlet that's powered by a lightning bolt."

"Is that all?" he asked with a wry smile.

Movement drew our attention to Hades and Persephone. She was helping him to his feet and there was a vacuum-like suction as he drew in a massive amount of power from the ground beneath him. By the time he was fully standing, he looked strong and confident enough to kick some chaos demon ass.

"Megiste," said Hades after being prompted by his wife. His brow stitched together as he searched his memory. "We've met before, haven't we?"

"Yes, Lord Hades. In passing, a long time ago."

He harrumphed at that. "Don't bother with all that *lord* shit. You're the Titans' savior, right?"

I harrumphed equally hard. "Savior is a strong word."

He smiled. "And yet I have you to thank for yanking me loose from my prison within a prison."

"That was Selene, I was just a conduit."

"Regardless," he said, taking a step forward and clasping my hand. "We are in your debt." He put his arm around Persephone. "Whenever you're ready to cash in, say the word."

"I don't want to be a party pooper," I began hesitantly, "but we still need to get rid of the actual chaos demon pretending to be you. There's a masquerade going on upstairs as we speak."

"Perfect," he said, not bothered in the least. "I can finally make those assholes pay a real tithe. Fight alongside me, or get the hell out of my house." He kissed his wife on the forehead. "Maybe we can stop throwing these damn parties all together."

She just smiled and patted his chest.

"Are you ready? Do you need more time to recover?"

He shook his head. "Not at all." His expression darkened as his anger took over. Persephone gave him space and motioned for us to do the same.

Hades's voice was barely more than a growl. "I'm going to end him."

CHAPTER FOURTEEN

Meg

Flames erupted at his feet, an indigo that sparked and crackled, stinging my skin just by being in proximity. Hades himself didn't change size or shape, but his mere presence took up a massive amount of room. Remi's arms circled around my waist and pulled me backward as the men moved to the wall.

Power built around Hades until it pressed against me with such weight I thought I'd be able to accurately describe what being at the bottom of the ocean felt like. As if moving in slow motion, he looked at us and nodded, black flames where his eyes had been.

Hades led the way out of the dungeon, and we followed at a distance. As we reached the main floor, couples were dancing to the music, their drunken laughter giving way to shocked silence or startled screams when the lord of the underworld appeared in their midst, pissed off and ready for battle. A path cleared before him, and I scanned the crowd for any sign of not-Hades.

Andrus was the one that spotted him as the demon stood in a corner, speaking with the man I'd run into earlier that night.

Without hesitation, Hades gathered a fireball and blasted it at the imposter. People dove out of the way, but the demon just stood there, letting the fireball hit him. It engulfed the creature in fire and while it burned, Hades addressed the crowd.

"Good evening!" he shouted. "It seems like we have a bit of a conundrum on our hands. You can stay and fight with me against this chaos demon, or you can get the fuck out of my way."

The flames had cleared and the demon, while looking a little singed, didn't appear that put out by the attack. I don't know what I was expecting. Maybe the demon would argue, and it would turn into a farce, each of them trying to prove they were the real Hades?

But instead, the demon shrugged, not even attempting to keep it up. Before our eyes, it dropped the face it had stolen and turned into something... *else*.

Its true shape burst out of its skin like popping a sheet of bubble wrap. Slick greenish-purple flesh sprouted oily brown hair that hung in lank clumps until most of its body was covered, just some bare patches on the face and chest. It was humanoid, standing on two legs, but a hunch on its back made the creature bend at a severe angle. Its limbs were gnarled and thick with sinuous muscle that looked like individual ropes bundled underneath its skin.

The face was flat, bat-like, with slits for nostrils and thin lips that disappeared when it smiled around needle teeth stained red.

People screamed and pushed for the doors. Servants scattered, joining in the mad dash and soon we were left alone with the chaos demon and his mysterious friend who hadn't moved an inch since the ordeal started.

"I'm glad we'll never have to host another of these worthless parties, but I thought at least a few people would stick around," said Hades. His flames still burned bright and confident, but his shoulders sagged a fraction, and his eyes regained their normal appearance.

"I haven't even introduced you to our guest yet," said not-Hades. He looked at me. "I told you I had someone you'd be excited to meet."

Taking that as his cue, the man standing next to the demon stepped forward, removing his mask.

No.

The face looked a bit different, the body was definitely bulkier, but the longer I stared the more obvious it became.

It was Bel.

My mates cursed, moving in front of me, but I pushed past them.

"Meg," said Gareth, trying to pull me back behind them.

I shoved his hand away, eyes only for Bel. "How did you escape?" I demanded.

Bel smiled and sauntered forward a few more steps. "That's not much in way of greeting. Hello, Megiste."

"Who helped you?" I asked again, determined to get answers.

Bel's eyes narrowed, and his smile grew tight. "The praise for that goes to my friend here. I'm sure you've heard by now that I've... upgraded. Legion offered some great enhancements, not the least of which is a connection to all the other chaos demons. Dendra here offered me a way out. Pulled me through time in a way that allowed me to not get shredded to bits. For which I am very grateful."

Dendra. A lesser chaos demon. We might have a chance after all.

"You just don't know when to quit, do you?" Remi asked.

"Why quit? There's no reason to quit when you're clever. I'll always find a way to continue this mission until you and the Titans are destroyed. I'm not settling for locking them away permanently. Each and every one of them will die. And now I'm confident that I have that power. Or I will, very shortly. There are still a few kinks I'm working out."

I took a risk and turned my back on Bel and Dendra. "Crazy idea, but I'm going to throw it out there," I said, drawing my five companions into a huddle. "What if I call the Hounds for backup?"

My mates didn't even balk at the idea, but Hades was hesitant. "That's still only the three of them and the six of us. Against two chaos demons, one of which is a hybrid Ætherim."

"Then what about Death?" I asked, studying Hades's face closely. "He mentioned the two of you weren't on the best terms anymore, but considering the circumstances..."

Instead of being angry, Hades only looked confused. "I'm not sure what he would be referring to. Unless things started to go downhill after that thing took my place." He shook his head. "I have no problem with Death. If you think he'll come, go ahead and call."

I sent out the call the instant he gave me the go ahead, feeling it echo through time and space.

Bel only smiled. "The Hounds couldn't beat me the last time we met. What makes you think adding Death to the mix would change the outcome?"

Dendra was suddenly choking, dropping to his knees. He hit the floor with a boom that shook the walls and rattled all the cutlery on the tables.

"Hades, if you would. This is your house, it should be your coup de grace."

Death was standing just behind the fallen demon's body, hand still outstretched from draining the energy from the creature. As Hades moved forward to deliver the killing blow, Death turned his attention to Bel.

"Your ego has always gotten you in trouble. I told you I wasn't going to interfere directly, and I still mean that. In most cases. But this is the second time you have antagonized me. The second time you have foolishly thought I was to be trifled with. You have a knack for making powerful enemies that you have no chance of winning against. There is no force on earth that is greater than Death."

He half-turned toward us. "Except maybe Hope." He turned back to Bel. "But she has long since abandoned you, my friend. The only things keeping you company are delusion and narcissism. And they are lousy friends to have."

Bel struck, a poorly aimed curse that swung wide and blew a hole in the stone wall. His form glitched for a moment, sort of fuzzed out at the edges, before becoming solid again. Whatever he'd been trying to do, he didn't seem put out it didn't work.

A flaming sword appeared in his hand, a weapon I'd only ever seen him use once before. It could cut through anything, and he swung it down at Death, who, to my eyes anyway, appeared to stand half Bel's height.

Death flickered out of sight before reappearing behind Bel and grabbing a hold of his arm. Bel roared, dropping to one knee as Death drained the life force out of him.

"It's over," said Death.

Bel grinned through his pain and his eyes met mine, the look in them not fearful, but anticipatory. I heard my mates cry out in shock before an arm banded around my waist and lifted me into the air with a crushing strength that squeezed the air from my lungs.

It was Bel. Another one. He must've separated himself, but how had we not seen the double? My mates attacked, and I drew up my stone skin and claws. I sank my claws into anything I could reach but had to stop fighting as Bel's massive hand clamped around my neck, poised to break it.

"Stop, all of you," he said.

I could feel my mates' tension and fear, but I could only catch glimpses of them as they circled, waiting for an opportunity to attack. Death released Bel's other form and took a step back.

"Typical," said Death. "Using a hostage to save your hide, like a true coward."

I shot him a look, not really sure his tactic was a good idea just now, but said nothing. Bel's grip on my throat tightened and I winced.

"You can call me whatever names you'd like. It doesn't matter. All that matters is that I'm walking out of here."

Meg?

I started. Remi. While Bel and Death continued their standoff chat, I replied. *I can hear you.*

Can you feel Legion? he asked.

I didn't know where he was going with this, but I trusted him. I tried to focus around the hand gripping my neck, getting a sense for the signatures in the room. Remi was right. Bel may have absorbed Legion, but the demon was still resisting, just a small splotch of spirit in the back of Bel's mind.

There he is. I can sense him, I said.

Try to draw him out. Maybe he can help you fight Belsioch from the inside.

It was an out-of-the-box idea, but those were usually the ones that saved us. I reached out for the signature, in much the same way as I would go looking for any of the Six. Crossing the distance in that empty, gray in-between and calling out to Legion.

The chaos demon was weak, barely holding on, but when he answered, I could feel his anger.

Do you think you can wrest control of Bel's body? I asked. *Even just for a second.*

I don't know. I can try.

If I give you a bit of my power to draw on, will that help? It wasn't an offer I made lightly. There was no guarantee he wouldn't try to possess me, or keep that link going even after I tried to sever it.

Yes, he answered.

With a quick prayer to the Fates, I forged a tenuous link to Legion with that fine silvery thread that I'd used like a fishing lure so many times while hunting for the men that would turn out to be my mates. I sent a small amount of power through it and Legion lapped it up.

Bel growled as he sensed something happening. "What are you doing?" he asked, shaking me.

Legion lurched forward and Bel's body spasmed as they fought for control over it. His hold on me loosened and I wiggled free, dropping to the floor where Gareth scooped me up and rushed me out of the way.

We all watched as Legion and Bel fought for dominance. Death took advantage of the confusion and began draining Bel's life energy again, but it wasn't working at the same speed. Legion must've been interfering somehow, fighting as much for his survival as he was to get free of Bel.

I tried to sever our connection. No go.

"Shit," I said.

"You can't drop the link?" Remi asked.

"He keeps adding more threads." I tried to erect some kind of barrier, but nothing was working. Legion kept latching on, sucking the energy out of me.

"What link?" Andrus glanced back-and-forth between me and the odd sight of Bel fighting himself.

"I had to give Legion some of my power in order to allow him to fight back. And now he won't let me sever the link." Dizziness washed over me as Legion siphoned a large pull of power.

"Death!" Gareth shouted. "Help!"

He only had to take one glance before he figured out what was happening.

"Why the hell did you link yourself to him?" asked Death.

"Hindsight," I said, my voice getting weaker. "Yell at me later."

Death's magick swept over me but he cursed. "It's not going to work. You have to do it yourself."

"Didn't you just say—" Remi started, but Death cut him off.

"There are limits to everything. If I'm the one that severs that connection, I could kill her. I'm not a surgeon, I'm the guy with the big stick."

"Meg, what can we do?" asked Andrus.

I shook my head, panicked. He was drawing too much power, I could barely think.

"Let me help," said Hades.

I could only nod. Gareth set me down gently and Hades went to work, reaching along the link and severing it one tiny thread at a time.

The stronger my connection with Legion got, the more I could tell the battle was turning Bel's mind to mush. It was breaking apart every bit of his identity, destroying him from the inside out.

Then, somehow, Legion triggered my connection to time.

"No!" I shouted, right before a wrenching pull snatched me up and hurtled me through time.

When I opened my eyes, it was to an unfamiliar scene. I was in a palace. Outside the window I could see mountains topped with snow. People dressed in thick furs against the chill bustled around the grounds. The hallway I was in was quiet and around the corner, I heard footsteps approaching.

A young man turned the corner first, followed immediately by several more young people, and an older man. The man was dressed in a formal fashion, but not anything so fine that would indicate he was nobility. The younger folks were all dressed in casual, high-end clothing, with fur collars and heavy material.

They were all talking animatedly, the young man in front seeming to lead the pack, gesturing wildly with his hands, a huge smile on his face.

I threw up an illusion around myself to match the clothing they were wearing, and stepped into their path. "Excuse me," I said, "can you tell me—"

They just brushed right by me. Nobody even glanced in my direction.

Did I put too much of an illusion on myself and make myself invisible? I readjusted and jogged to catch up.

"Pardon," I said, much louder this time, staring at the older man in the back of the group.

Nothing.

I dropped the illusion entirely and reached out to grab his sleeve, but my hand passed right through him.

"What—" I stopped dead in shock. What was going on? And where was I?

Chapter Fifteen

Bel

Legion was tearing into my mind, shredding into my memories. I felt my grip on reality loosen. This was all that bitch's fault. Every time she meddled, every time she got in my way, something went wrong. After everything I did for her, she kept ruining everything!

The demon was drawing an immense amount of power, and the second I lost my grip on Meg, my bargaining chip was gone. But maybe Legion did me a favor. With any luck, they would kill her at the same time they defeated me. Or at least would expend so much of her power that she wouldn't be able to recover. She could see how it felt to lose everything and be a weakened mess, barely hanging on to life.

They were becoming careless, throwing everything at me like a wild animal cornered. *That* feeling I could relate to. If I could just hang on, just a little longer—

What is that? What is he doing?

Where—

Rage bloomed and I roared. Destroy.
Destroy!
I must win...
How did it all go wrong?

...where am I?

"You can't be serious?" I said, eyebrows raised. "You can't think that's any more rational a solution then just burning the whole place down and starting over again."

"Sometimes the easiest solution isn't the best one, Master Belsioch" said Bran. As my longest standing tutor, I cared for the man's opinion, but dammit can he be a self-righteous bastard.

"I don't understand why we're even discussing this. Why focus on the hypotheticals? There are enough things to worry about in this kingdom without you getting lost in scenarios that may never happen."

My lip curled as I looked at my sister. Her rationalism never ceased to bring down the conversation.

"Well, *Ardiel*," I said, hitting her name with annoyed emphasis. "Some of us like to have stimulating conversation just for the sake of it. Why don't you go back to our father and share your thoughts with him instead? You two always seem to be of the same mind anyway."

"I can't," she said. "He's in one of his moods. Otherwise, I would be. I learn a lot more from him than I ever have from you."

"Is he off destroying a town again? Laying waste through the countryside? Poisoning water supplies?"

Ardiel didn't respond, so I must have been close. "What set him off this time?"

She shrugged. "Probably something you did. You do realize that every time you defy our father, he finds something else to break instead of your face." Her eyes narrowed. "Maybe I should do it for him. It would save everyone a bunch of time and hassle."

"You wouldn't dare," I said, issuing the challenge. We stared each other down, neither of us willing to budge, but of course, I cracked first.

The second the corners of my mouth turned into a smile, my little sister pumped her fist in the air in victory. "Undefeated champion! You're such a pushover."

I laughed. "I let you win." My tone turned serious. "Is Father really off on a tear again?"

Ardiel frowns. "Yes. And Mother won't leave her rooms. They must've had a fight again."

Anger on my mother's behalf welled up inside me. She put up with so much from that bastard, and for what? Before I could sink too far into my reflecting, someone called my name.

"Bel!"

I turned to find Egulund running after us, Cassius and Jurmond in tow. I grinned at the sight. "Where have you been? You were supposed to have been back hours ago." I leaned in conspiratorially. "What kind of trouble have you been getting into?"

"We'll tell you all about it, later," Egulund promised with a wink.

My sister groaned. "Why do you hang out with these idiots?"

In response, all three of my friends made a huge show of acting wounded. "Why do *you* say such hurtful things?" Cassius asked.

"I'm just pointing out the inherent flaws of my brother's choices."

We turned the corner, and I glanced out the window at the mountains, pulling my fur collar tighter around my throat. This may be an outer promenade, but my father should still have put glass in these windows.

"Where are you heading?" asked Jurmond.

"There are some merchants that came by with some rare plants from out east. My mother and I have been designing a garden. I thought I would surprise her with these."

"Such a sweet boy," Cassius mocked, clapping his hands next to his chin and batting his lashes. I rolled my eyes, but couldn't stifle my laugh.

"At least I've done something for my mother besides make her question her decision to have children," I retorted.

I heard the drum of hoofbeats below but thought nothing of it. We'd passed out into the courtyard, and I saw the merchants across the way, one cart laden with verdant plants. A wonderful thing to see in the dead of winter.

"Belsioch!"

I winced and my sister gasped. Our father had returned.

"That was quick," I mumbled to Ardiel under my breath.

She gave me an apologetic look as Yarovit stalked toward us.

"I'll get the plants and hide them somewhere," she said, grasping my hand before hurrying away.

"Thank you." I stopped and waited for my father to approach. My friends went with my sister to secure my long-awaited prizes.

Bran stayed. "Majesty, I'm glad to see you have returned safely."

"Leave," my father said to Bran.

Bran bowed his head and left to join my sister. Coward.

"I was just at the front. Do you know what I found?"

I gave him a deadpan stare. "I can't imagine."

The blow to my ear almost sent me tumbling to the ground, a high-pitched squeal filling my head. My father grabbed me by the arm and dragged me to the stables, calling for one of the stable hands to prepare a horse for me, and a fresh mount for him.

"We're going back. And you're going to finish the job I explicitly gave you."

I took the reins offered to me, but I didn't mount my horse. "I did what was necessary. Your *orders* didn't make sense."

He grabbed me by the collar of my tunic, lifting me so my toes scraped the ground. "It doesn't matter if they make sense to you. I gave you orders. And I expect them to be followed. To the letter."

"The job still got done, didn't it?" I asked, refusing to back down.

Still lifting me in one hand, he punched me in the stomach with his fist so hard I felt something rupture. "Keep talking, boy. I can dole out a whole lot of punishment before I risk killing you." He leaned in so close our noses almost touched. "And as soon as I sire another whelp on that bitch mother of yours, I *will* kill you."

Anger flared, and for a moment I'm touched by madness, pure and simple. I struck my father with every ounce of force I had, my punch landing dead center of his chest. I enhanced it with my budding magick, so it packed enough of a wallop to force him to drop me and stumble back a few paces.

The fire in my father's eyes was worthy of any god of war. I crawled backward on my hands and feet as he advanced, drawing his sword. This was it. He was going to kill me this time.

He swung, and I closed my eyes. I didn't want to see it coming. I felt the rush as the blade swung down, but then it stopped. The cold press of steel against my neck made me open my eyes to see my father's face splitting into a cruel grin.

He sheathed his sword, throwing back his head and howling with laughter. "You are a coward! You weak little pissant!" His laughter faded into dark chuckles. "Looks like I'll have to teach you all over again how to be a man." He jutted his chin back toward the palace. "Go pack your things. You will come with me to the front line, and we will stay there until you can be a son I'm proud of. Or you won't be returning." He sniffed. "Then who will protect your whore mother. Your sister? I will give her to one of my warlords. Maybe several."

I said nothing, just nodded my head and did as he said. He'd follow through on every one of his threats if I gave him a reason. I just had to find a way to end him first. If not for my sake, then for my family's.

I snarled, pushing Legion back. Time stopped spinning and I was able to orient myself for just a second, regaining control of my mind. I had to get him out. We were in some kind of in-between place and when I looked over, I saw Megiste looking just as stunned as I was.

"You! Make this stop!" I ordered.

Then everything lurched and we were swept up again.

I've been on this post for hours, staring out into the dry, hard-packed landscape, as the icy wind bears down on me. I refused to wear the fur cloak I've been offered by my father. Even though I've given him few reasons to mock me over the last decade of fighting by his side, at any given time his actions could be a test. Rarely was it ever an act of kindness.

Far in the distance, I clocked movement, a caravan. I let my mind wander to thoughts of what they might be carrying. Maybe something exotic. Something from a faraway land. Gifts for someone to deliver to a family member as a surprise.

I never found out if my mother liked those plants I secured for her. I hadn't been back home since the day my father nearly killed me, changed his mind, and took me with him instead. The only consolation was that he hadn't been back home either, so for now my family was safe.

And in the meantime, I watched, and studied, and waited for my chance to get even. Turn the tables and make him fear for his life.

It was just a matter of time before I got my chance.

"Bel, you're done. Go get some food," said Marchon, clapping me on the shoulder.

"Relieved already? But my toes have barely begun to freeze," I said, raising my eyebrows in mock surprise.

"If you want me to come back later, I can," he said, turning to leave.

"Never mind, it's all yours."

My tent was freezing when I returned, the fire having gone out and someone—one guess as to who—left the flap open. My father pissed on the ashes, too. A great joke.

I managed to get my hands on some fresh bread today, along with some winter fruit and hard cheese. Far better rations than I've had in weeks.

The sound of soft footsteps stop outside my tent and someone cleared their throat. "Bel?"

My heart leaped and a smile sprang instantly to my face. I set aside my dinner and went to meet my love.

I threw the tent flap back and pulled her in, closing it behind her. Palming her cheeks, I tilted her face up to steal a quick kiss. "What are you doing here?" I asked.

"My father had to make a delivery, so I tagged along. I can't be gone long." Norah smiled, running her hands over my chest before pushing me firmly away. "So don't be tempting me," she teased.

I only met her a few months ago, but she's become my entire world. A chance meeting one night as she was filling in for one of the kitchen maids at her father's tavern. Some of my compatriots got handsy and I stopped it. The rest is history.

"When do you think you can get away again?" she asked.

I shook my head. "We're expecting trouble coming this way. Raiders from the north have been seen closer to the city. Which reminds me, you should go stay with your aunt in the country for a while. If we can't stop them, they'll hit the city first, and I don't want you there."

"I have full faith that you'll stop them in their tracks."

"Norah—"

"But I will go to my aunt's house," she said. Her serious look broke into another of her radiant smiles, and I drank it in. No matter what hell battle offered, she was the one thing that made it all worth it. I wouldn't have met her if I hadn't been forced to accompany my father here.

"Thank you. I will send word when it's safe."

"Come tell me yourself," she says. "I will turn any messengers away at the door unless it's you."

I grinned. "You would make me dessert my post? My soldiers?"

"I would make you run away with me," she said, and for a minute, every part of my being was tempted to do it.

I clasped her hands. "Soon, I promise. I just need to secure my family's safety first."

She knew that was code for killing my father, but she didn't bat an eye. She'd met the man, and she'd heard the stories. He'd have killed her if he ever found out there was something between us, for no other reason than to spite me.

"I have to go," she said, leaning in for another kiss. "I will depart tonight."

I checked outside my tent to make sure the coast was clear before sending her off. My heart ached to watch her go. Before she turned the corner, she looked back one more time, gifting me with one more of her smiles before she disappeared.

CHAPTER SIXTEEN

Bel

Everything hurt. Confusion. Sorrow. Make it stop. Had to get Legion out.

No.

No, not again. Sick to my stomach.

Carried away by the winds, drowning in the waves.

Make it stop.

"What's on your mind?" Norah asked, sitting beside me and threading her arm through mine. "You normally don't stay in here this long unless there's something serious happening."

I smiled and kissed the top of her head. I've been sitting in my mother's garden for half the day now. It was still beautiful, but not as lush and verdant as it was when she was alive.

No matter how carefully I laid my plans, or how ardently I tried to protect her, I hadn't been able to save my mother from my father's wrath.

I should've seen it all coming. My shortsightedness got her killed.

But that was years ago, and I'd buried him the same day I buried her.

"I'm going to have to leave soon. The Titans are moving in. If we don't put up a united front against them, they'll wipe us all out. The Ætherim are drawing lines, but the Titans refuse to play along."

"But they're Titans," said Norah. "How can you hope to win against them? Why don't you just give them what they want?"

I sighed. "Then where does it end? I have a responsibility, my love. To my people, to the other members of my pantheon. If we just roll over and get out of their way, there's no telling what they'll do."

Norah was silent for a long moment, staring into the pond.

The koi were always my mother's favorite. She had plenty of stories from when she was a child, spending hours in the emperor's gardens with her attendants, feeding the fish and splashing in the water.

"When do you have to go?" she asked.

I rested my hand on Norah's belly, already filling out, and let the guilt rush in. "Tomorrow."

Her breath shuddered but she kept up a strong front. I wrapped my arm around her. "I'm sorry I couldn't give you more warning. I tried everything I could think of to avoid this."

"You're a king. That's what kings do. Whether their wives like it or not."

"I will come back to you. The Titans are powerful, but we are greater in number."

There were tears in her eyes, but she didn't let them fall. "I know. I believe you."

Watching the palace disappear into the distance, I forced myself to focus on the road ahead. I couldn't let myself be distracted. We'd gotten word the Titans were heading this way, about a day's travel west. If we met them somewhere in the middle, we'd be far enough away from the city that it should remain safe, no matter what the fallout.

"What do we do when we get there? Have you heard the stories?" Bran asked. The minute I'd taken my father's place, I'd appointed Bran as my advisor.

"I've heard them."

"Just the sheer size of them. How do we fight that?"

"Are you getting cold feet on me now, Bran? Regretting your advisory position?" My tone was cold. I had no patience to suffer cowards.

"No, Majesty. This is all just beyond my scope of expertise. Warfare of this kind—"

"Is unheard of. Nobody has much experience in it, so it's new for all of us. We need as many heads on this as we can get, but if you're not going to be of any help, run along back to the castle. You and your shame can keep an eye on things there."

He blanched. "My apologies, Majesty. I will gain control of myself. I won't let you down."

"You better not. I intend for us to make it back. Don't make me a liar."

A rumbling began so suddenly the horses shied, rearing up and dumping half the riders on the ground before bolting. I kept my seat, reining in my horse and turning in furious circles to find the source of the disturbance.

Ahead, not a mile away, a small group of people, maybe two dozen in total, were walking along the wide road. As they came, they were growing in size.

"Ætherim to the front!" I bellowed.

I jumped down off my horse and waited for the rest of them to join me, motioning ahead as the Titans closed in on us. "Take your full forms," I said, already shedding my human guise.

"Already? But we'll lose power too quickly. We can't take full form in this realm without the earth reclaiming our power as fast as we can draw it. We need to lure them into the Strange-fells," said Atum, a young Egyptian god I'd only just met.

"If you have an idea on how to do that, I'm listening," I said. Nobody had any response.

"Full forms," I repeated, continuing my transformation. There were a hundred of us in total, and with those kinds of numbers, we stood a chance.

The Titans were massive, easily three times our size at our full manifestation. But this would be where we held. I would not let them anywhere near my home, my city, or my family.

I stepped forward, taking the lead as we met the Titans in the middle of our field of battle.

"Turn back," I said. "Either cede, or go. You are not welcome here."

Kronos, a terrifying figure bigger than all the others, stepped up to meet me. "We are not seeking parlay. We want an end to this madness. If you will not back down, you leave us no choice. You and your ilk cannot be allowed to continue in the manner that you've been ruling. Too many innocents are getting hurt. Dividing yourselves into pantheons is ridiculous."

I gestured behind me. "There are Ætherim of multiple pantheons here. We can still come together when the threat is great enough," I said. "You are the ones making something out of this that isn't there. We rule fairly. Have you met humans? Their mortality makes them reckless, foolish. Their efforts to make their names known, to have their legends be sung... they need guidance, and sometimes that takes a heavy hand."

"Guidance? You aren't guiding these people. You use them as fodder for your games. You hunt them as food. Your guidance is tantamount to the Ancients that we worked *together* to lock away. All you've done is take their place, and made nothing better. It is your immortality that makes you foolish and reckless and power-hungry. You see yourselves so much higher than the people you claim to lead. It's not right."

"We're at an impasse then," I said, drawing back to the Ætherim's ranks.

Kronos gave me a grim smile and a nod.

I gave the order to draw swords, and in unison, every enchanted blade was pulled from its scabbard with a whisper on leather. Each weapon was imbued with the holder's magick that made it transform in size along with the bearer and acted as a focus to direct our power. To see a hundred such weapons across the field was a sight that gave me hope.

The rest of the soldiers, all Strangers of various disciplines, fanned out around us as cavalry, pikes, and polearms ready to be a thorn of annoyance and distraction to the Titans. Every little bit would help.

Selene clapped her hands and the sky darkened, plunging us all into a moonless night. Cries of surprise echoed from the troops below, but the light emanating from the Ætherim in our full forms is more than enough to illuminate the scene.

"Shields!" I called, initiating my own. A new wall of light added to the steady thrum of power overtaking the entire field.

The battle was long and arduous. Rhea unleashed her power over the earth, opening great fissures to swallow our foot soldiers and cavalry, and our gods of earth counter.

Oceanus coaxed water to rise from the aquifers and combined his power with Atlas's to churn the ground into a sluice, opening up massive pockets into empty air and plummeting darkness. We lost several Ætherim before we could reverse it.

Kronos hit people with concentrated blasts of time, evaporating them into nothing. Most of our shields couldn't withstand it. He was a problem that would have to be solved foremost.

I split off from the main group with my most loyal cadre. Kronos was standing apart from the others, on a rocky outcrop from which he could watch the battle. With the kind of power he wields, he could wipe us all out, but he's holding back. Why?

With quick, careful steps, battle raging behind us, we circled around to stage our attack. I crept up the hill, sending my cadre around to cause a distraction. Setting myself in position, I motioned to Cassius and Jurmond.

They hit Kronos with fire and air, churning a flaming tornado around him as I leaped in my attack. They break the flames as I crashed into the Titan, toppling him and flipping him onto his back. My sword was at his throat in an instant, but he blocked it, his face stoic, almost serene.

"Why do you hesitate?" I asked, pressing back with all my strength to force my blade nearer to his throat.

Kronos stared at me, pitying. "Having great power means knowing when to use it and when to stay your hand."

He spoke to me like a grandfather giving worldly advice and that only made me angrier. I bore down on him, close to cutting his throat, and he was trying to teach me a life lesson?

"Power isn't everything," he continued. "You knew that once. What happened to you?"

Red flashed across my vision. "You don't know anything about me."

"You have a family to go home to. If you call your forces down, and agree to the stipulations we want to set to your rule—"

I shoved the sword closer still, breaking through his resistance. "No stipulations, no surrender," I growl. "My father was right about that."

Kronos met my eye and I hesitated. No. That man was a monster, I know that. Why would I—

I shook it off. My blade was only inches from his throat now. It wouldn't kill him, but it would take him out of the fight. We might contain them if given enough time to construct something.

"Think about this," he said. "This is your last warning."

His hand lit up with another of his concentrated time attacks, the purple energy crackling. He put even more power into this than the others I'd seen him use. I could feel the heat of it singeing my skin.

But I wouldn't give up. If I landed this blow, it might kill me, but it would also give my forces a chance at victory. I pressed forward.

Kronos sounded almost regretful. "Very well then."

His magick sparked and roared to life as my blade finally drew blood. He released his devastating attack and my entire world flashed purple.

And it faded. Everything came back into focus, and I was still on the battlefield, Kronos still pinned under my sword, staring back at me with sad resolve.

A hush had fallen, and I realized my blade was badly damaged, half of it melted away. Turning to the field to see what caused the hush, my eyes followed the trail of damage.

Kronos's attack glanced off my sword and deflected. There was nothing but rubble all along the path of destruction. How many had been hit?

Everyone's gazes were fixed farther afield, and I realized what brought the battle to a halt. A strangled cry left my throat as I leaped to my feet, jumping off the outcrop and running toward my city.

The only thing left to mark its existence were a few crumbling walls and scorched earth.

The palace was gone.

My wife—

I fell to my knees, bellowing with pain. Tears cloud my vision and for a moment I thought I could see a woman with silver hair and violet eyes standing off to the side, but she vanished.

They were gone. My entire city was gone.

Nothing even left to resurrect.

I doubled over with grief, punching the earth as I realized I'd never see Norah again. Our child would never be born. My chest felt like it was caving in on itself, and I threw my head back in an agonized howl, my throat shredding from the force of it.

My teeth clenched.

Kronos.

My hands fisted in the dirt and I sank onto the ground, losing track of everything else. The battle could have waged on, and I wouldn't care. But the silence remained. I was alone.

I shuffled into the ruins of my city, hoping to find something or someone that survived, but there was truly nothing left.

His fault. This was all Kronos's fault. They were dead because of him.

I collapsed with exhaustion in the vicinity of the palace, once again in my human form. I'm drained and overwhelmed with grief. I couldn't even cry anymore.

No troops returned, none of the Ætherim appeared. They'd left me to suffer alone.

Days passed. Weeks. I couldn't move.

Part of me wanted to end it, but I knew Norah wouldn't approve. She'd have wanted me to keep going, keep fighting.

So that's what I did. I kept fighting until I exacted my vengeance. I let rage drive me. There was nothing else I cared about anymore.

Kronos and his ilk would pay. I'd take my revenge, and it wouldn't be quick. They'd know every bit of grief I suffered and feel it a thousand times worse.

Vengeance was all that mattered.

My father was right about that.

CHAPTER SEVENTEEN

Meg

I watched in stunned silence as Bel grieved. I'd had no idea. His gaze passed over me for a moment as tears clouded his vision, and I thought he'd actually seen me.

Then his gaze moved on.

As I watched the battle from a distance, I'd been too distracted to notice that time was leveling out. But I realized I was regaining my sense of equilibrium.

"So this is where everything started," I said, I'd thought to no one.

"Fitting," hissed Legion.

My pulse spiked at the surprise, and I spun, stalking toward them. "What did you do?"

They gave a noncommittal shrug. "Tried to fight for my freedom."

"Did you trap us in his memories?" I asked, but immediately discounted it. "But we're also traveling through time, so that doesn't make sense."

Had Legion discovered another quirk of my gifts? Bel's physical body had to be somewhere, and I felt the timestream moving around us, so we were in *a* reality. But nobody could see us.

That thread connecting me and Legion also seemed to have broken. At least, they weren't drawing power from me anymore.

I could ponder that later. I needed to figure out how to get back. "Detach yourself from him and get out of here. Clearly his grip on you is slipping."

"His grip on his sanity is slipping."

I shot him a look. "Can you get free or not?"

"Already done. My form was all but destroyed." They looked at me keenly. "I don't suppose there's any chance—"

"Fuck off," I said. "Find your own way home."

Legion didn't wait around to see if I would change my mind. They disappeared to somewhere unknown.

Part of me wanted to help Bel, even knowing what he would become. I had no idea if he would be lost in his memories, trapped in his mind. If his body would be lost in the in-between spaces. I wasn't even sure I could find his physical body if I tried. If his mind was shattered, his signature might be too. There would be nothing to trace.

He might still be a threat after this, or he wouldn't be, but either way, I needed to get out of here.

I took one last look at Bel, on his knees, tears streaking through the dirt on his face, and I left.

I only did a quick sweep of the gray purgatory in the middle of time and space, just wanting to return to my mates and knowing in my gut that I wouldn't find Bel there.

To me, it seemed like I'd been gone for days, but when I dropped back in to Hades's palace, I fell right into the middle of a verbal war.

"We have to go after her," said Gareth.

"I'm not sure what kind of magick that was," said Death. "I have no idea how to track her."

"You're the one with the connection to Time," Andrus said to Gareth. "You figure something out."

"I would if I—"

"Okay!" I called. "I'm okay!" All three of my mates whirled toward my voice, surrounding me like a shield.

"What happened? Where did you go?" Remi asked.

"It's a long story," I said.

"Which you can tell once we're out of the underworld," said Death. "Clock is ticking. And don't forget that we left Felix with a giant toddler."

Just the thought of moving along to the next task so quickly made a headache bloom behind my eye.

Hades pulled Persephone close. "We owe you a favor. Don't hesitate to ask."

"I'm glad we could help," I said, leaning on Remi. I knew he of all my mates wouldn't make a big deal about it and get the others worried.

Death hesitated and looked at Hades. "How long would you say that you were either under the influence of, or replaced by that chaos demon?"

Hades shook his head. "I'm not sure. By the best of my recollection, I would say he showed up about... two decades ago."

"Ah," said Death. "That would make more sense then." He offered his hand. "Are we good?"

Hades took the proffered hand. "Certainly."

Death gave a small bow of his head. "Good. Glad to hear it."

A throat cleared, and I looked over to see Roshanna. She looked again like she had after our impromptu trip to the portal room. Her eyes were clear, and she was acting of her own volition again.

"I've reconsidered your offer," she said, giving us a shy smile. "Technically, I am part of Hades's household, but since I'm guessing the Hades I worked for is no longer around..." She looked at the real Hades expectantly.

He motioned with a wide sweep of his arm. "I'm not even sure who you are. You are most definitely free to go."

She bowed. "Thank you, Lord Hades."

"Are we done here?" asked Death, pointing at the imaginary watch on his wrist. He didn't wait for an answer, simply spirited us away.

In an instant, we were in the Strangefells, in a cozy house in the country. The twilight sky peeked through high windows.

"They already got the customary tour," said Death to Roshanna and me, "but welcome to my home."

I squared my shoulders, wanting to get the show on the road before I succumbed to exhaustion. And maybe I wanted to avoid confronting the feelings raised by seeing Bel's past.

Feel bad for the person he was, Meg, not the person he became.

Gripping Remi's arm, I said, "Let's get Arthur back."

Roshanna hung back awkwardly and I paused. "Um, I'm not really sure where you want to go from here..."

"I'll stay," she said quickly. "If that's alright? I can help out with anything you need. Just in general. I don't have any magick of my own, but I'm good with running a house."

Her face was still changing, returning to something resembling normal. Other than cheeks too wide, overly large eyes and swollen lips, there was still something familiar about her.

I looked at my mates as they waited for me to follow before turning back to her. "We'll talk about it later, yeah?"

She nodded. "Go on. Get your mate back."

I smiled and took off.

Felix was waiting with Arthur in a small sitting room. Arthur was wandering, eyes open wide with curiosity as he explored, running his hands over the spines of books, staring out the window.

"Has he been like this the whole time?" I asked.

Felix nodded, getting to his feet. He crossed the room and took me in his arms without hesitation, giving me a quick kiss which caught me by surprise. "I'm glad you're back," he said. And I could tell he meant it.

"Let's see what we can do," I said. I turned to Arthur, letting my eyes drink in the sight of him. None of us ever thought we'd see him again, and I had been responsible for that. And now here he was, in the flesh, just waiting for his memories to be restored.

"Help me get him settled," I said to Felix, who nodded.

Felix walked over and took Arthur by the elbow, guiding him over to a chair. "We're going to sit down for a minute," he said. Arthur just smiled amiably and did as he was asked.

I crouched in front of him, staring into a face that didn't have a whole lot of comprehension. He was a blank slate.

I called up a portal, seeking back in time to the place I'd first met him in medieval Germany. Sensing how exhausted I was, my mates crowded around me, giving me their support and boosting my power.

The portal opened on the lower castle hallway, the one I'd carried my laundry through. Arthur was walking away from the portal, but he sensed it and turned. "Megiste?"

He took tentative steps forward, and I beckoned him closer, reaching through the portal. He looked over my shoulder to where his identical twin waited. With a gentle smile, I offered him my hand. "It'll make sense in a minute. Just trust me."

As he got closer, he could see his brothers in the room as well, and his face split into a wide grin. He took my hand without hesitation, and I pulled him through, guiding him into his body and merging the two versions of himself.

Watching Arthur's eyes go from blank acceptance of the world around him to fully conscious and aware was a transition I don't think I'll ever forget. He leaped to his feet as his brothers-in-arms surrounded him.

I backed up to the side to let them catch up, wondering if he would have any memory of the time directly after this, when he was in Bel's torture dungeon and then became a wandering spirit.

I had no idea how it worked. There was so much trauma and it was such a short span of time, maybe those memories after I'd sent him away would be erased.

"Not just a washer woman's assistant anymore, eh?" he asked.

It took me a minute to realize he was talking to me. "No, not so much."

"Didn't I just part ways with you? I'm assuming that load of laundry was still usable?"

That answers that question. I took a deep breath. "There are a lot of things that we need to talk about. I don't want to hide anything from you, and I'm sure you have a few questions of your own." I looked at the others. "I'll give you a bit to catch up. Come find me when you're ready."

"You don't have to leave," he said.

"I have to prepare for this too. It's not gonna be an easy conversation," I said, bowing out and heading back to talk to Roshanna.

The group launched into catching Arthur up on everything that had happened. I wasn't sure what, if anything, they would say about his death and retrieval and everything that led up to it, but I was sure they wouldn't want to get any part of the story wrong, and would leave it to me.

When I turned the corner, Death was waiting with the former construct. They were talking quietly, and I skirted around the couch to take a seat across from her.

"What do you think about—" My words choked off in my throat. Roshanna had changed appearance even more, and I certainly knew her face.

"Sasha?"

CHAPTER EIGHTEEN

Meg

How could this be? What were the odds that Arthur's wife was sitting across the parlor from me? That the chaos demon posing as Hades just happened to change this woman into his construct servant?

I could only stare at her in a mixture of horror, shock, fear, anguish... This couldn't be happening. I thought the worst thing that would happen would be that Arthur's and my relationship would be haunted by the *ghost* of Sasha. But now the actual person was sitting across the fucking room from me?

This had to have been by design. But to what purpose?

"Meg? Are you okay?" she asked.

I blinked. "You don't remember who you are, do you?"

She shook her head, confused. "A construct for Hades."

"Care to explain for the people in the back?" Death asked.

I looked at Death, brow furrowed, already chewing on my lip anxiously. "This is Sasha. Arthur's wife."

Death groaned and looked around at her. "Oh, shit." He looked back at me. "What do you want to do about this?"

"What?"

He leaned in and spoke under his breath. "We go for a nice ride out to the countryside, look at some pretty flowers, make it nice and painless... Are you getting what I'm saying?"

I looked at him and backed up. "Are you crazy?"

"That's a matter of opinion," he said, grinning.

"We're not doing that." Sasha was watching us cautiously, so I leaned in again. "It's not her fault she's caught up in this," I hissed.

"What do you plan to do, then?" he asked. "I don't think I need to tell you how this is going to go down if Arthur—"

"Sasha?"

Arthur and the others had just walked into the room. Death closed his eyes and grimaced. "Well, that's that."

Sasha looked at him blankly. "Do I know you?"

Arthur was taken aback and looked at me for help. I sighed. "She doesn't remember anything before she was brought to the underworld."

He nodded, but still didn't look like he was following. He approached her, stepping lightly, afraid to spook her. "It's me. Your husband."

Sasha cocked her head, staring at him hard, before shaking it fervently. "No. That can't be right."

The rest of my mates were standing around watching with horrified expressions, mouths agape and unable to speak.

"You can fix it, right?" Arthur asked me. "You can do the same thing that you did for me?"

Felix stepped up. "Do you realize what you're asking?" His words were gentle, but still held a tone of reprimand.

"She's my wife, Felix."

The dark elf shook his head. "She *was* your wife. She's not anymore. She doesn't even remember you."

"Because of Hades. Or the chaos demon, or whatever he was."

"Doesn't this strike you as a bit coincidental?" Andrus asked, also keeping his tone light. "It has to be some cruel trick. She might not be your wife, just someone who looks like her. We've got chaos demons and mad Ætherim in the mix. There's no telling what any of them would be capable of. This is exactly the kind of thing they might do. Trying to put a wedge—"

"I don't care!" Arthur snapped. "There has to be a way to make sure. We have to try."

"I think Felix's first question to you was accurate," said Gareth. Unlike the others, he was not stepping lightly around his words. "Think about what you're asking Meg to do."

Arthur stared at Gareth, not understanding. It was Remi that elaborated. "Meg is your fated mate. And you're asking her to restore a woman who may or may not be your wife. She looks like her maybe, but you have no way of knowing. And the fact of the matter is, that woman is not your mate. Meg is. And this mission cannot go on if you aren't with us on this."

"There's a reason that the Titans warned us not to get too tangled up in relationships," said Gareth.

I looked at him. "I didn't know that."

He nodded. "This is a perfect reason why."

"It had been two-thousand years. How was I supposed to know that the entire plan hadn't failed? I fell in love. What would you have had me do?" Arthur asked. He pointed at Remi. "What about him? He had an entire family."

"That's not fair," said Remi, the tips of his ears turning red.

"How is it any different? Your story ended tragically, and my heart breaks for you, but my wife is right here." Arthur wasn't backing down.

Sasha was watching all of this in silent shock, her gaze bouncing back and forth between the men as they fought. When there was a lull in the arguing, she spoke. "I'm not sure what's going on, and I'm sorry if I've caused anybody any trouble. I don't know any of you. The first I met Meg was in the underworld. I may have had a life before then, but I don't remember it. And even if Meg could restore those memories, I'm not sure if I'd want her to. I just want a blank slate, a new start."

Then everybody's eyes were focused on me. "I'm at just as much of a loss as you guys are."

"My vote is still that this is some kind of trick," Andrus said.

"Just let me speak to her. If we get to know each other again..."

"Then you are setting your entire team up for failure," said Death. "You are putting all of your stability in jeopardy, the bond you all share."

Arthur took a deep breath. "A small amount of time. That's all I ask."

There was an explosion of indignant responses from my mates, Felix included.

"Okay," I said. I hadn't needed to raise my voice, but they all felt quiet.

"Meg—"

"It's alright. He should have a chance to make up his own mind."

Death tsked. "I know you're trying to maintain diplomacy, but you should think about this."

"We need to go get Hadi. While we're gone, these two can figure something out." I was so overwhelmed I could barely even form a coherent thought, let alone make a decision that might make or break Arthur's relationship with us all. I didn't have a right to demand that he cast Sasha aside, even if this was some kind of manipulation. He had to come to terms with that on his own. Otherwise, I was just trapping him with us.

I stood. "I need some time. Excuse me."

Without knowing where I was going, I hurried out. Hopefully Death didn't have any secret rooms or unsavory interests that I would be walking in on by barging through his house.

I'd allowed myself to think that this would be a happy reunion. That we would find ourselves back on track, ready to get Hadi and tackle the last leg of our journey. Of course it couldn't work out that way. Was that selfish of me? I just wanted a definitive win, something not marred by confused feelings.

I laughed to myself, a bitter sound. So many fucking confused feelings. After having Bel play with my head for so long, and then finding stability with my mates, and now it had all turned to drama and bullshit again.

I never thought this would be easy. A relationship with six men all of whom I'm supposed to be bonded to... there was no easy way to navigate it. Shit was going to come up, and often. But after Felix... this was just one step too far.

Ducking around a corner, I found a small room to hide in. I clapped my hand over my mouth to stifle my sobs, sliding down the wall until I thumped heavily on the floor.

My knees curled into my chest reflexively, and I wrapped my arms around them, burying my face in the raggedy remnants of my masquerade dress.

I made no attempt to staunch the flow of tears. I just couldn't bring myself to curb more of my emotions. I've been tamping this shit down for too long.

Maybe we could just get Arthur to accompany us to the gates of Tartarus, get the mission done, and then he could go merrily on his way. Those words sounded cold and bitter even in my head. I should be happy for him, right? I'm the one who separated them. Now he has a chance for his happiness again, to pick up where he left off. Why should I feel jealous? Just because the Titans had an idea in their mind when they made this plan, when they made me, didn't mean it had to go exactly as they wanted it to.

Things had been going wrong since the beginning. Either the Fates were slipping, or this was the hectic mess they wanted. Or maybe they just had an end result in mind, and everything in between was up in the air. Who was I to say boo?

None of this was fair. I never asked for this. I never wanted this drama. I'd been put in one impossible position after another, and it wasn't getting any fucking easier.

My feelings were boiling out of control. My mates must've been inundated, and I was surprised they were keeping their distance, especially Gareth.

I snorted. That man was hardheaded, overprotective, possessive... but he was also caring, sweet, deeply emotional and he would go to the end of the earth for me.

If Andrus had any faults, it was that he was too laid-back sometimes, too supportive. I laughed, swiping at the tears on my face. Fiercely attentive and devoted, down to earth, but also terrifyingly aggressive in defending those he loved.

Remi was... Remi. Once you got past the gruff exterior, he was an even bigger teddy bear than Andrus. Maybe a bit more nihilistic about things, but he kept us in check whenever we let our confidence and hope for the future get too overinflated.

Felix. I knew Felix was a good man. There were hints of it everywhere. I think somewhere down the road he just decided not to show that side of himself, and he'd buried it deep. He let it show in other ways, like his loyalty and his devotion to his brothers. And I was grateful that he didn't force something on our relationship that wasn't there. He was honest, and that's all I could ask.

And I certainly couldn't hold it against Arthur if he wanted to continue his relationship with Sasha. What the Titans demanded of these men was too much. To rip them away from the brothers they would give their lives for, drop them individually across time where they would never meet each other... They could say it was a safety measure, to protect them from the Ætherim's vengeance, but they were putting them in an impossible situation at the same time. And to forbid deep, personal relationships for what ended up being a couple of thousand years? That's cruel.

That kind of time may be nothing for the Titans, but without that bond of service that the men swore to them, none of my mates would've been immortal. Long-lived, absolutely. But the Titans could never comprehend what they had been asking of their Six.

All of us were brought together on this collision course developed over centuries, guided by the Fates, culminating in an all-but-impossible task we had yet to face, and interrupted every step of the way by forces directly and indirectly trying to sabotage us.

This wasn't fair to any of us. And while my mates had signed on for this, I hadn't been given a choice. I was assigned a task, given a very poor road map, enough money for bus fare to the next city, and a kick in the ass on the way out the door.

Tiredness dragged at me. I was finally starting to calm down when there was a knock on the door. With one more quick wipe of my face, I said, "Come in."

CHAPTER NINETEEN

Felix

As Meg hurried away, I wanted to go after her. She was trying to hide it, but I could see how hurt she was. And the farther she got away from us, I could *feel* how much she was breaking. How could things go so wrong at every turn?

"Excuse us," growled Gareth to Sasha, steering Arthur away as the rest of us followed. As soon as we reached a room down the hall, he shoved Arthur inside and shut the door behind us all. Just then, a stab of pain tore through all of us, and I gasped.

"Gods," said Andrus, face drawn with worry. "Meg."

"After everything else she just went through, and now this?" said Remi.

"What happened in the underworld?" I asked.

"Hades wasn't Hades. He and Persephone had been kept in the dungeon while a chaos demon had taken Hades's place."

"What?" I asked.

"And in the final battle, somehow, Legion began to fight against Belsioch and latched onto Meg, tapping into her time-travel ability somehow. She was dragged away with them to gods only know where. She couldn't even talk about it when she came back."

"Then she didn't even take any time to process it and went right to work bringing Arthur back," I said, marveling at the selflessness of this woman. Why had I treated her so badly? She never meant anybody any harm and was going out of her way to help, even when she was the one that needed it more than we did.

Gods, I was an idiot. Were my past experiences with women really affecting me that badly?

More sadness and grief rolled over us. She was so overwhelmed, she couldn't hide it from us if she tried.

Gareth looked at the door, wanting to go find our mate, but he rounded on Arthur instead, not disguising his anger in the least. "What do you think you're doing?" He pointed blindly in the direction we'd come from. "Do you honestly think that's your wife? This is clearly a ploy, designed by Belsioch or any of the other enemies we've made so far. And even if it was your wife, she doesn't remember anything. You don't even know if there's anything left of her that you would recognize in there. She's mortal, for gods' sakes! I'm sorry that you didn't have more time with her, but she should've been dead a long time ago. That's just a fact. Are you going to stand there and jeopardize the entire mission the Titans tasked us with?"

"You know what my power is. Or have you forgotten?" Arthur's words were quiet, almost a whisper.

Gareth bristled. "Of course I haven't. What does that have to do with anything?"

Arthur looked at Gareth like he was pitying an ignorant child. "I'm blessed with divine luck. Everything around me works out exactly as it should. Exactly as I need it to. As *we* need it to. Who's to say I wasn't supposed to be reunited with Sasha? Maybe she has some part to play in this yet."

"Are you hearing yourself right now? There's no way you could have been consciously using your magick. You were dead! You couldn't have twisted any luck in that state, and that chaos demon created 'Sasha' at least a couple of years ago anyway. Plus, she's mortal, which means she's been dead for quite some time. You said you were both together in medieval Germany, right?"

Arthur narrowed his eyes. "Yes."

"So her soul was kicking around, losing all attachment to her former life before that chaos demon brought her back in that creepy reincarnated form. Which is again to say, it's clearly a trap."

"We can't know that for certain. I just need some time to talk with her. If Meg could just restore her—"

I could only stare at Arthur in astonishment. "Are you kidding?! What has gotten into you? This isn't the Arthur I know. Even if Meg did agree to such a thing, Sasha herself told you she didn't want that." I looked at the others. "Did something go wrong when Meg brought over his old self?"

"I don't see how," said Gareth. "It seemed to go the same as it did when she used it on you."

"You need to see this rationally," said Remi to Arthur. "I'm trying to give you the benefit of the doubt, because you don't know Meg yet, except for the brief interaction you had with her before. Do you have any idea how guilty she felt for how things went down with you? It was eating her alive. Every time she had to reveal the role she played in your death to one of us, it destroyed her just a little bit more. And she will always go out of her way to try and right her wrongs. She would deny herself peace if it meant making up her transgression to you."

"What are you talking about?" Arthur asked.

Andrus hissed. "You don't remember that do you? What's the last thing you *do* remember?"

"Helping Meg pick up her laundry basket after I crashed into her in the hall. Just moments before that portal opened up."

He looked around at our grim faces.

Should we tell him? Would she want us to?

Remi cursed and Gareth paced. "This just keeps getting better," he said.

"Someone feel free to explain what's on your mind," said Arthur.

Once again we all exchanged looks. "I don't think that's a story for us to tell," I said. "Meg needs to be the one you hear it from." When I first learned of everything that went down between Meg and Arthur, I was shocked and hurt. But when I heard the explanation from her, I could tell how much her guilt was eating at her, and how regretful she was for letting Belsioch play her like that. Arthur needed to hear that too.

Gareth agreed. "Let's give her a little more time. She's starting to calm."

"You can feel her emotions?" Arthur asked.

"Of course," I said. "We're bonded mates. Did you forget how those work too?"

Arthur may have been my best friend and a closer brother than any of the other men around me, but that also meant I was far more likely to escalate fights with him than the others were.

"What's happening with her right now?" he asked, not looking any of us in the eye.

"She's hurting," said Remi. "She needs our support, and we're here, trying to remind you how common sense works."

"Can we all just agree that the lot of us lived very different lives while we were apart?" asked Arthur. "I'm trying to understand where you're coming from, but I also ask you do the same for me."

I shook my head. "And here we kept telling her that you were the best of us." I couldn't stomach this anymore. I threw my hands up and left the room.

"Felix," Arthur called after me.

I ignored him.

CHAPTER TWENTY

Felix

Even though I was probably the last person she wanted to speak to, I found myself drawn toward Meg. Before I could talk myself out of it, I knocked on the door of the room she'd hidden in.

"Come in," she called. I could still hear the tears in her voice.

"It's me," I said, cracking the door open. "Do you mind if I come in?"

She gave me a tired smile. I saw the tear streaks on her face and the puffy redness of her eyes as she tried to wipe away the evidence and put on a brave face. My heart clenched. I sat down next to her and pulled her into my arms.

"I'm sorry," I said.

"For what?" she asked, leaning her head against my shoulder. I was surprised as I felt some of her stress ease away. Was she finding comfort in *me*?

"What you're going through. This is just one more blow against you. You haven't even said what you experienced when you were ripped away with Legion and Bel."

"They told you about that?" she asked.

"Not much, mainly because they didn't know anything. You don't have to tell me either if you don't want to." I slipped my hand over hers, twining our fingers together.

For a while, she was silent, and I was content just to sit there with her.

"It was the strangest thing," she said. "Bel's mind was being ripped apart while he was fighting Legion for dominance. It's like we traveled back in time, but when we got to the destination, nobody could see me. And then I realized that it was Bel's past. Maybe those were the times that made the most impact on him, so as he was struggling against Legion, maybe he was using those anchor points." She shook her head. "I really don't know."

Meg jammed the heel of her free hand into her eye. "I'm just so tired." Her voice cracked, and fresh tears welled up in her eyes. "So fucking tired."

"You're allowed to be. You have been doing your damnedest to hold us all together, and you can only be a rock for so long. It's okay if you need support, too. And I'm sorry I contributed to the problem."

She chuckled. "You were honest. Even if it wasn't an easy truth for me to hear."

I squeezed her fingers. "I may not have been as truthful as I thought."

Her stare bored into me before I met her gaze. "I've been reevaluating things. It might have something to do with the fact that Death looks like one of my exes. But it's made me think about what might be motivating my relationship with romance."

She raised her eyebrows, intrigued, but didn't push for further details, for which I was grateful. I could barely even explain it to myself yet.

"When I was stuck in Bel's past, it was like I was seeing all of the vignettes of how he became who he is. His father was a monster, he was a mama's boy, the love of his life was taken from him, mostly because of his own actions, but the Titans were involved. I'm sure he blamed them for it. I was seeing a whole side of him I never knew about." She gave a dark chuckle. "I was in a relationship with that man for fifty years, and I never knew him at all."

"Do you feel bad for him?" I asked.

She shook her head. "I thought I did. I feel bad for the person that he was. For the boy that was abused by his father. For the man that saw his entire life fall apart in the blink of an eye. He seemed to be a good, honorable person. There were just too many things piling up, and he couldn't stand the thought of losing. And then when he did lose such an important part of himself, all he could think about was vengeance. I'm not excusing what he did, or what he continues to do, but I kind of—understand him now."

"What happened to him? Is he still attached to Legion?"

She shrugged. "I think his body is out there somewhere, but I don't know what state his mind is in. Legion should be long gone, and in no shape to take any kind of action against us either. But Bel is an unknown." She frowned. "Not an ideal circumstance."

We lapsed into silence for a little longer.

"Did anyone tell you how Arthur and I ended up being so close?" I asked.

She shook her head. "No."

"Arthur was taken from the Strangefells as a baby, switched at birth with a fae child."

"A changeling?" she asked.

I nodded.

"As they do, the faeries that took him grew tired of their pet and put him out on his own. Abandoned him in the forest. I'm not sure how familiar you are with the lands of the dark fae..."

She shook her head. "I'm not really." She laughed softly. "I've always been too afraid to go there, honestly."

I smiled. "That's because you're a rational person." Memories of that time in my own life were spotty at best. I'd discovered faerie wine in my youth and that was that. But meeting Arthur was a life-changing event.

"I was hunting a stag. I'd tracked it to a clearing and I had my bow trained on it when I sensed another person nearby. Not fae, which was unusual. Most of the time, if you find non-fae in the Dark Forest, it's by stumbling across their dead bodies. They don't stand a chance against the beasties that reside there. But this one... this one was very much alive."

"Do you remember how old you were?" she asked.

"Not more than a hundred. Arthur was only in his twenties."

"And he was surviving in the wilds of dark fae territory?" She shook her head in disbelief.

"My thoughts exactly. I postponed my hunt to check out the interloper and spied on him. He seemed oblivious that I was there but when I took one step too close for his comfort, he shot an arrow within an inch of my head. Purposefully missing. Just turned and shot, without even taking time to aim." I snorted. "His bow was so crudely made by his own hands it wasn't until many demonstrations later that I believed that first shot was intentional. The arrows weren't even straight, but he'd figured out how to set the fletchings to make them fly right.

"After that meeting, I would track him down every time I was in the woods. It wasn't long before we forged a friendship. He didn't trust any of the fae after being treated so cruelly by his captors. But we found common ground, and I convinced him to join me at court."

"Finvarra's?"

"No. I belonged to a smaller court, neither seelie or unseel-ie."

She cocked her head in interest. "I didn't know that was a thing."

I grinned. "Not many people do. Most of the time, we still pay allegiance to one of the main courts, but we're left to govern ourselves unless things get rowdy."

"It seems like rowdiness is a prerequisite for fae, especially the dark fae."

"And what glorious mischief we make," I said, my grin widening at the slight blush that tinged Meg's cheeks.

"Arthur had to beg the queen for residency. There are trials, a series of tests, usually the psychological sort but sometimes it involves battling monsters. If he wanted to stay, he had to pass them all. But I begged a boon from her so she'd allow me to go with him and see him through."

"What happened?"

A cloud passed over my face at the memory. "It got... diffi-cult. Turns out it wasn't a boon after all. She just wanted to put two people to death creatively for her and the court's entertainment. We survived, clearly, and the queen was so shocked she bestowed Arthur with his magick."

Meg blinked. "He wasn't born magickal?"

I shook my head. "No. Since he seemed to possess no small amount of luck, she gave him a command of it. He can twist anything in his favor. Also why he's such a pivotal addition to our group."

"I had no idea," she said, worrying her bottom lip with her teeth as she considered this new information.

I didn't want to break the sense of ease we'd found, but this was as good a time as any to bring it up. "Arthur wants to know about everything that happened after—"

She sighed. "Yeah." She leaned her head back against the wall and cast her eyes to the ceiling. "I know I need to do it, but just the thought of it... especially with Sasha around..." She looked at me. "I felt horrible after Arthur and I were making out right after we met. For betraying Sasha like that, letting myself get swept up in—" She gestured helplessly, knowing I would understand but still frustrated she couldn't find the words. "Now here she is. It's a chance to make things right. But dammit if I'm reluctant to do it. Am I terrible for being jealous?" Her cheeks reddened at the admission. "I know I have no right to be, but especially when he barely even gave me a second glance before asking me to restore his wife... that stung."

She stumbled on her words, discomfort taking over the truth she so badly wanted to get off her chest. "I don't blame him, I mean, I—just because of the whole mates thing, it doesn't—"

"You have every right to feel what you're feeling. Nobody can say otherwise," I said. I lifted my hand to her cheek and grinned. "I know a little something about self-indulgence. It's very therapeutic to just let yourself feel. And maybe I got a little carried away sometimes..." I looked at her out of the corner of my eye, and she laughed.

"I could use a little self-indulging hedonism right now," she joked.

Now *that* was something I could give her. A chance to get lost in the here and now before she had to dredge up more pain and face more difficult choices.

Her violet eyes met mine as I ran my thumb along her cheekbone. "If that's something you'd like, I'd be more than happy to oblige."

Meg's breath caught at the promise in my eyes, but she shook her head. "I'm not into pity sex."

That caught me by surprise. "Who said anything about pity?" I took both her hands in mine. "I have felt many emotions toward you, but pity has never been one of them. Confusion, anger, no small amount of fear."

She laughed and bowed her head, but I caught her chin gently and tilted her face back up. "And plenty of wonder and gratitude that you gave me another chance, even after I was such an ungrateful dick."

A heartier laugh burst from her chest at that. I leaned in and kissed her. "I'll keep being truthful with you every day we're together. *This* is the truth. I don't know if I can love you the same way the others do, but I see how devoted they are to you. And I understand it now. No matter what, you *do* have my devotion. You're an amazing woman. I can't believe the shit that you put up with. And I hope that you're willing to keep putting up with mine, because I have no intention of going anywhere."

Hope welled up through the bond and I smiled, resting my forehead against hers. "Let me take away some of your pain, even if it's only for a little while."

Meg pulled away hesitated, chewing her lip. I could feel her response before she said it. Lifting her head, she said, "Please."

I reached up and caressed the tips of her ears, and she shuddered. "Sensitive, aren't they?" I asked, voice husky, before capturing her lips with my own. The kiss began as a consuming smolder and deepened to an inferno.

My hand moved behind her neck, crushing her to me as our tongues tangled. A prick on my lip made me pause and I realized Meg's fangs had appeared.

"Sorry," she breathed, flushed.

I licked at the blood, smiling, before working at the ties on her corset. The knots were tied tight and I settled for tearing it open. Meg shimmied out of her dress as I dispatched my own clothing. Her hands roved over me, nails scraping and teasing. I leaned her back and recaptured her lips before making my way down, giving each nipple close attention, teasing them to taut peaks.

The noises she made when my teeth grazed the sensitive skin on her stomach had me making a mental note to think of special attentions and toys I could introduce to fully take advantage of the newly discovered erogenous zone.

I grasped her thighs and spread her legs slowly, watching her face with a wicked gleam in my eye. My fingers grazed her clit but kept on going, pushing two into her opening and hooking inward. I pumped my fingers, loving it as her breath hitched, her head lolling back.

A lance of pleasure that reached through the bond had her back arching and she moaned, reaching for me. I knew exactly what she wanted and I pulled my fingers away, leaning down and replaced them with my tongue. As I probed at her opening before traveling upward and swirling around her nub, she gasped and clenched her thighs around my head, twining her fingers in my hair.

My tongue dove into her slick entrance and she was quickly ratcheting toward climax. My fingers circled her clit and she bucked her hips against me, a long moan escaping her throat. I gripped her thighs, holding her to me tight as she cried out.

I switched out my fingers in place of my tongue and pumped into her faster, hooking them at sharper angle. Another orgasm tore through her right on the heels of the last. I backed off, massaging until her shuddering came to a stop. I nuzzled my face into her belly and she pulled me to her, kissing me deeply as she tasted herself on my tongue.

Still panting, she pushed me backward and gripped my cock, licking the tip before taking me in her mouth. Her tongue swirled around my shaft as she worked her way down, easing her throat open until she was swallowing my entire length. She bobbed, watching me watch her. My breathing became shallow, and I stopped her.

"Ride me." My request was husky, and she climbed on top of me, straddling my hips. She gripped my hands and stretched them up over my head, leaning forward until her body was flush against mine. Sliding herself up and down, I moaned as she teased my cock with her wetness without taking me inside her.

When I couldn't take it anymore, she leaned back and languidly rose, grasping my rod and guiding me into her, sinking onto me with a satisfied sigh. My hands slid over her hips and she mewled as she rode me, using my breath as a guide to her pace, picking up speed when a growl ripped from my throat and my fingers dug into her hips.

"All fours," she said roughly.

I did she asked, repositioning behind her as she settled on her hands and knees. I groaned as I worked all the way in, her pussy clenching around me. I pumped slowly a couple of times before spurring my pace, her moans filling the room and driving me on harder.

I reached down to stroke her clit, building her up as I tensed. Meg unraveled with a shattering cry, and I followed close behind.

When we finally came down, she lay next to me, catching her breath. She cast a dubious glance at the dress piled in a shredded heap on the floor. "I might need to borrow your shirt."

CHAPTER TWENTY-ONE

Meg

Explaining everything to Arthur was easier after the stress relief I'd received from Felix and a quick but hot shower. Arthur himself took the information well, all things considered. It was probably a blessing that he didn't remember what Bel had done to him.

"I'm sorry if I put you in a difficult spot, earlier," he said.

I forced a smile. "You have nothing to apologize for." I considered him. "If Death is okay with it, I think it might be a good idea if you stay here with Sasha while the rest of us go to get Hadi. You should have a chance to talk things out."

He gave a weary smile. There were dark circles around his eyes, and he wasn't any more immune to the stress of this situation than the rest of us. "Thank you. I don't want to cause an issue between all of us, but if there's any chance, I owe it to her."

I nodded, trying to keep my face neutral. "It's understandable."

"And thank you for braving the underworld to bring me back," he said.

"It was the very least I could do." I stood. "We should get back to the others."

Everybody was waiting in the main room, along with Sasha. She kept trying to catch my eye, share a smile. With her memories as they stood, I was the only one here that she knew. But my lingering guilt and doubt made it difficult to give her more than a brief nod, which only made me feel more guilty. Too bad the Gieses couldn't have succeeded in beating sociopathy into me. Emotions were really the pits sometimes.

"I'd like Arthur and Sasha to stay here," I said to Death, keeping my fingers crossed I wasn't overstepping my bounds. I certainly didn't want to abuse the hospitality of the most powerful egregor in existence.

He looked surprised. "I suppose that would be fine."

I let out the internal breath I'd been holding. "Thanks." I turned to the rest of my mates. "The rest of us are heading to Thebes. Let's bring Hadi home."

My entire body buzzed with anticipation as we stepped through time onto the lush eastern bank of the Nile. Of all places in history to visit, ancient Egypt was my favorite by far. The land was breathtaking, magick was thick in the air. Every inch of this place was steeped in mystery, ceremony, and grandeur.

Shallow-bottomed riverboats paddled lazily by, their days over as the sun moved to the horizon. The air smelled hot and damp, the rich soil beneath our feet still warm from the blazing sun. Tall grasses were being cut back as people worked the fields, planting seeds.

I took a moment just to settle in. Let myself be surrounded by the calls of people in the distance, the rush of water, tree frogs croaking, long-legged ibis birds standing in the shallows, their feathers rustling.

"I've always loved Karnak," said Remi, staring off in the direction of the temple complex just visible in the distance. "The atmosphere here is just... something all its own."

I nodded in agreement. The gargoyle had a soft spot for places to commune with higher powers.

None of my other mates had much to say, being too busy looking around, awestruck. After a while longer of basking in the vibrant setting sun, Andrus said, "I've only been to Thebes a couple times. After Karnak peaked, but before it's decline."

"The closest I've been is Alexandria," said Felix.

Gareth remained silent. I could sense an unease from him, but he was keeping it carefully controlled. The flock of ibis birds took off with a cacophony of warbling cries and a rush of wings.

"Where to?" asked Felix.

As I tuned in, I found that Hadi's signature was easier to pick out than the others had been. "Wow," I said. "He's not even trying to stay under the radar. Either he's pumping out a lot of power, or I'm getting better at homing in on signatures."

"Hadi is a dragon. He doesn't do subtle," said Remi, frowning.

"Wing span envy," whispered Felix, leaning close. My surprised laugh spooked more birds out of a nearby tree and I slapped my hand over my mouth.

"This way," I said. We followed the bank of the Nile past small docks, huts, and irrigation channels. Smaller temples were dotted along the way. I found an avenue through the fields and headed away from the water toward the hustle and bustle of the city.

An irrigation ditch was hiding behind tall grass, and I almost stumbled right into it, but Felix grabbed my hand before I fell.

"Thank you," I said, getting ready to jump over it, but Felix stopped me again.

"Take a look," he said, pointing.

I peered into the water, cast heavily in shadow. Then I saw two eyes staring back at me just above the waterline.

"Nile crocodiles," he said. "Vicious jerks."

"Hey!" a man called from across the field, making his way toward us with a full head of steam. "You can't be here!"

"Sorry!" I called back, switching seamlessly into Late Egyptian. "Our friends stranded us and took off in the boat. We're heading back to the city."

The man finally reached us. He was dressed in well-worn clothing, caked in the grime of a long day. "Stay out of the long grasses, fools. The crocodiles have been swarming of late."

I glanced back at the irrigation ditch. "I see that. Thank you for the warning."

He eyed us suspiciously. "You say your friends stranded you? What were they doing on the water today? You don't look like fishermen or ferrymen."

"Uh, we might've borrowed my father's boat," I said shyly.

He shook his finger at us. "You should know better. This is a sacred day. Only people with legitimate business should be working. Everyone else should be preparing for the pharaoh's arrival."

I cast my eyes down and acted properly abashed. "Yes. You're right. We shouldn't have been so careless."

The man pulled a face and waved us off. "Get going. And watch out for crocodiles. I've had to listen to too many feeding frenzies of late."

The look of horror on my face was genuine and I nodded emphatically. "Thank you."

We hurried quickly away, sticking to open areas where we'd have plenty of warning to see them coming. "You think they're swarming because Hadi is pushing out so much power?" I asked.

The four men actually looked stumped.

"I've never thought about that," said Gareth. "It's an interesting idea. I can call normal wolves to me."

"Reptilians stick together," said Andrus with a grin, and I gaped at him.

"Damn. You've got the lexicon down pat," I said.

"Reptilians?" asked Felix. The others had moved into the language of Egypt's New Kingdom easily, but Felix must only have a tentative connection to my language skills. He was using a mix of Ancient Greek and Latin, studded with Late Egyptian words.

"Lizard people," I said, pausing and turning to face him at the sight of a grin spreading across his face. "Don't you dare tell Hadi I laughed at that." Dragons weren't known for their lighthearted sense of humor.

Felix nodded and took my hand as we continued on our way. As we neared the edges of the fields and the city of Thebes was fully in view, I took a moment to enjoy it.

High sandstone walls, ornate hieroglyphs and obelisks, brightly painted likenesses of the gods, and bright white lime-stone-washed buildings were stained orange by the setting sun. People were streaming into the city, and I could see the beginnings of fires springing up outside in preparation for the festivities. Cheers and laughter filtered toward us on the air and I could smell delicious foods being prepared.

"What's going on tonight?" asked Gareth.

I sought around in my mental library of history. That man had said something about the pharaoh's arrival. People were planting, so the Nile's annual flood waters had just receded. I wonder...

"Let's keep walking. I have an idea, but I'm not sure yet. We're getting close to Hadi, though."

The closer we got to Karnak, the more the butterflies in my stomach flapped. I'd never traveled here to see it with my own eyes. I almost let out a squeal of excitement when I saw the Avenue of Sphinxes all lit up with brazier fires along the length, stretching south into the distance.

"This must be the Feast of Opet!" I said. Blank stares were my only answer. "It's one of the biggest festivals of the New Kingdom. After the Nile floods there's a huge procession for the pharaoh down the Avenue of Sphinxes to celebrate fertility and to make the king's divine reign official for another year. They travel from Ipet-Resyt in the south all the way to Karnak. I've always wanted to see it!"

I was bouncing up and down on the balls of my feet, unable to contain myself. My mates were grinning at me, but not because they shared my enthusiasm. "Fine, I'm a nerd. So what?"

Andrus laughed. "This is a whole new side of you I haven't seen."

I eyed him. "I was pretty damn excited to see Athens in its glory days. Despite the Persian army that was coming to burn it down."

A sudden image of Philomena came to mind, the high priestess of Athena's temple who refused to leave her post. She was prepared to give her life for her devotion. I hoped she didn't suffer in the end.

All of that seemed like so long ago now. Years, decades even, when in fact it had only been about a month since the real mission had kicked off.

Remi frowned. "Should we be expecting some kind of cataclysm or invading army? That seems to be the common theme."

"Don't jinx us," said Gareth. He'd turned serious again, watching the activity around us with a keen eye. Was he expecting something?

"We'll be fine," I said firmly. I was ninety-percent sure. Okay, maybe seventy-percent. "We're getting close."

We joined the throngs of people walking the avenue, looking for a spot to set up and watch. The avenue itself would be cleared for the pharaoh's procession and the pack of people was already tight all along the roadside. Finding a place to view the street would be tricky.

I scanned the area, keeping my eyes on something closer to Karnak. I didn't know how many people would dare to get that close, so it might be a good place to settle in.

Priests were standing at the great gate into the temple, lined with obelisks and ornate pillars. "Let's try to get closer up here," I said, pulling Felix along behind me.

"Are you sure we should get this close?" he asked.

"Those priests don't look welcoming," said Andrus.

"It's fine," I said. "If all else fails, we can cast a full illusion and they'll never know we're there. We might never get a chance like this again."

They agreed, for which I was grateful.

The closer we got, the more the priests eyed us, but they said nothing. Not yet. I led us to the first open area past the crowd, where only a few others were milling around. Wealthy citizens were seated in lacquered chairs nearby and I was thankful that Felix had made us look at least somewhat well-to-do.

"This is really happening," I said, staring around me, soaking in the sights. I wasn't even looking for details and faces like I should've been.

The crowd swelled as the sun went down, and soon I could hear the drumbeats and singing as the procession neared. An eager hush fell over the crowd as we waited for them to appear.

Dancers came first, followed by musicians. Exotic animals and their keepers, the pharaoh's court, and finally the pharaoh himself, being born in a wooden barque carried by servants and surrounded by three smaller, golden barques. The contents were hidden from view, but they must have been the statues of Amun, Mut, and Khons.

It was everything I'd dreamed to see. I couldn't tear my eyes away. Not until the bond began to sing with the recognition of people reunited did I realize my mates' attentions were elsewhere. I forced myself to look away from the avenue to follow the gazes of the men.

In the middle of the pathway leading up to the gates of Karnak stood a priest in a white-linen pleated kilt with a leopard skin draped over his shoulder. His bald head shone in the firelight and his presence was immense. I would put him about the same size and body type as Gareth, but the power he was pumping out rolled over me. He was staring right at us, his mouth parted in surprise. One priest leaned in to whisper something and Hadi, for there was no mistaking that's who this man was, nodded and reluctantly turned back to the procession.

He raised his arms above his head and his bronze skin erupted in flames. My breath caught in my throat as the entire crowd fell silent in awe. Hadi moved forward, still ablaze, to greet the pharaoh as the procession came to a halt.

There were no words exchanged for the crowd at large to hear, but the ritual proceeded and the group moved into the temple. Hadi cast a few more glances in our direction before they disappeared from view.

My mates turned back to me. "That's our guy?" I asked, my mouth gone dry. I wasn't expecting one of the Six to be in such a central role. High priest? And he was flaunting his power without a care in the world.

They nodded and Remi was shaking his head in answer to my unspoken question. "Dragons."

CHAPTER TWENTY-TWO

Meg

We waited for an hour until the pharaoh reemerged, a loud cheer exploding from the people. They filled in around the procession, not getting too close to the pharaoh or his entourage, but dancing as the music started up again. The feasting would begin as the days-long celebration came to a close for another year.

I watched for Hadi to appear, but he didn't.

"What do you know of this ritual?" asked Remi. "Should he be back out here by now?"

I shook my head. "I don't know. It would seem like he would've returned with the king, especially when he was putting on a show like that."

"We should find him," said Gareth. "The sooner we leave, the better."

That tension I'd been feeling from him earlier returned and I put a hand on his arm, drawing him away from the others. "Is everything alright?"

Gareth glanced at his brothers, but they were still looking out for Hadi.

"The last time I was here, I might've crossed paths with one of the Ætherim. Maat."

I raised my eyebrows. "Goddess of justice and judgment? The one who weighs the hearts of souls after their deaths and feeds those found unworthy to her pet beast, Ammit? That Maat?"

He nodded. "This isn't her central territory, but—"

"I take it the encounter didn't end well?" I asked.

He shook his head. "It wasn't like that. I was here on an errand from the Titans. She found me *too* worthy." He scratched his head. "She took a bit of a shining to me."

My eyes widened before laughter bubbled up and I couldn't stop the giggles. He looked at me helplessly. "She's very... aggressive with her affections. And she doesn't like to be turned down. I don't want her to find me and have it become a whole thing." He looked at me. "And I don't want you making a new enemy because of me."

Fair point. I didn't want to deal with an angry goddess either. Especially when that goddess had a giant hell beast at her command that ate souls as a primary food source.

"Let's find Hadi, then," I agreed. "The temple itself should be empty. As far as I can tell, he's still in there. It shouldn't be hard to find him."

Andrus had taken the time to plot the best way into the temple to avoid being seen but before he could explain it, Felix tossed an illusion around us that made us disappear. Andrus scowled. "I could've gotten us in just fine."

"Now we won't have to risk it," said Felix, shrugging. "And we can try to sneak up on Hadi." His mischievous grin was back.

"You want to sneak up on a dragon?" I asked. "Do you want him to burn the place down with us in it?"

Felix shrugged. "He'll probably hear us coming."

"Probably," muttered Remi, who was taking up the rear of our little expedition.

It was hard to maintain my focus surrounded by all the sights I was being presented with. Once we stepped among the carved and painted pillars with their lotus tops, passed the obelisks erected by previous pharaohs to leave their marks on the world, entered through the main gate and into the temple proper... I was overwhelmed. It was so stunning it almost brought tears to my eyes.

Fires burned around the complex in ornate braziers, and I gazed up at the carved faces of Hathor that appeared on at least half the pillars in the main hall. The roof above us had slats expertly positioned to allow for the view of certain constellations on important dates. The air would've been close and hot if not for the desert breeze that carried along the vents cut in the walls, just enough to cool the sweat on my skin.

I could hear water trickling up ahead, and as we made our way into the heart of the temple, a fountain appeared. We stepped out into a small courtyard, the oldest part of the structure. This was the temple that the entire complex had sprung up around. The magick was condensed, ready to spring when summoned.

Water flowed around it like a mini Nile, and I could see the glow of a fire within the inner chamber. For us to be here was forbidden at the highest level of ancient Egyptian law. If we were caught—

Being a Stranger had many benefits.

We stepped quietly over the footbridge and entered the heart of the complex. The golden barques were here, returned to their proper places by the king as he reavowed his divinity.

"I could have you executed for stepping foot in here."

The low voice rumbled through me, and I turned. Hadi was sitting on a bench against the far wall, partially hidden in shadow. His deep brown eyes, tilted upward at the corners, stared into me even though he shouldn't have been able to see me, lids hooded under perfectly arched black eyebrows.

Felix grumbled and dropped the illusion. "It was worth a shot."

The flames weren't roiling around him anymore but that didn't mean he was giving off any less power. He was devastatingly handsome, more striking than Felix with his fae beauty.

I was speechless. Gareth stood at my shoulder, his wolf already wanting to fight for dominance. "Hadi," he said. "It's been a while."

The dragon nodded, his full lips curling into a grin. His eyes never left mine. "That it has."

There was no elated reunion like the others had had with each other. They all stood and appraised each other in silence, seeming to have some sort of silent conversation or test of wills.

"So... we should go?" I asked. As loathe as I was to leave this place already.

They continued to stare at each other. Power rose between Gareth and Hadi and I realized almost too late that they were about to challenge each other. I stepped between them, facing Hadi. The dragon's gaze evaded mine, continuing to seek the wolf as he stood, taking a step toward Gareth.

"Hey!" I shouted, putting my hand flat against Hadi's chest. The two of them were devolving so fast, giving in to their alpha animals that I'm not sure either of them fully recognized me. Gareth had transformed into his partial wolf form and Hadi... it was hard to wrap my mind around it. His head and neck elongated into a dragon's, talons erupting from his hands and ridges of scales and spikes appearing down his arms and legs. A tail slid to the ground and coiled to strike. His scales were pearlescent white, each one edged with the shimmering blue-green, like the inside of an abalone shell.

I pulled my stone skin around me just as Gareth howled and Hadi roared, claws raking with me caught in the middle. I slowed time as Andrus and Remi moved to intervene while Felix rushed to the outer edge of the temple to get behind Hadi. They were all moving in slow motion as I swept Gareth's feet from under him and twisted Hadi's arm behind his back, kicking the back of his knee to force him down.

Time slipped back into its normal pace and three confused faces and a cantankerous wolf turned to me as Hadi struggled to free himself from my grip. Thanks, enhanced strength.

"Calm, the fuck, down," I said, staring Gareth down. Embarrassment rolled through the bond as he regained his control.

Hadi's anger only grew as he fought me, and I feared he might change into his full form. A grim image of the lot of us squished into pancakes against the close walls of the temple came to mind, Hadi's head and tail poking out of the opposite doorways. It was so absurd, I busted out laughing.

Instead of stoking his anger further, Hadi stopped dead. His reptilian head cocked to the side and the slitted green eye on the side of his face that I could see blinked, the clear membrane sliding over first before the outer lid followed suit.

"I'm not letting you go unless you stop this machismo bullshit," I warned.

A rumble and a huff of hot air puffed from his nostrils before he dipped his head. I let him go and he slowly stood, not changing back to his human form. He was even taller like this, and he towered over me, his neck craned down so he could hold my gaze.

I reached out to run my fingers along the scales on his arms, receiving a pleased growl in answer. My stone skin faded, but I called out my wolf's claws to make a point. Hadi's pupils dilated as he noticed them and his tail wrapped around my leg, pulling me closer to him and away from Gareth.

But Gareth didn't react. I shot him a grateful smile before turning back to the dragon. "Whatever the hell that was, it's not going to happen again."

Hadi lifted his head to Gareth, but I grasped his lower jaw and turned his head back to me, firm but careful. "You're talking to me. Not him. The alphas have no place in this conversation."

Hadi raised his hand and gripped mine, moving it from his jaw. His tail tightened around my leg like a python and we stared at each other for a full minute before he blinked. His tail loosened and he moved my hand to his cheek. The scales were cool to the touch and smooth as glass. I stroked my thumb along his cheek and he leaned into my touch.

The next instant I was looking at Hadi in his human form again. He pulled me close and kissed the palm of my hand. "I am sorry," he said. Then he looked past me at Gareth and the others. "To you as well."

The tension that had been lying thick in the air finally broke and the others moved in around us, welcoming Hadi back to the fold at last.

CHAPTER TWENTY-THREE

Meg

"Are you ready to leave?" I asked Hadi. "Is there anything you need to wrap up first?"

Andrus shook his head. "This doesn't feel right. We have time to give someone a chance to wrap up loose ends without being chased out by an invading army, threatened by a volcano, hunted by an angry god, or foiled by a chaos demon."

Hadi's eyebrows peaked. "What's that?"

"We'll explain everything when we're back at Death's house," said Felix.

"What?" He stared around at us, waiting for one of us to crack and admit it was a joke, but no such luck. He tipped his head. "I look forward to the stories, then." He paused. "I would like to take one last look outside."

I nodded and Hadi moved into the courtyard, tilting his head up to look at the sky.

Gareth moved up next to me, but he resisted touching me. "You don't have to hold back anymore," I said, smiling. His arm wrapped around my waist in response. I turned to him, placing my hand on his chest. "Thank you for letting me solve the problem on my terms."

"I'm not sure I let you, as much my wolf was shocked into submission at the sight of you holding a dragon in an arm-lock." He smiled. "You're terrifying." He leaned down to kiss me.

"That was a sight," agreed Remi.

"How did you manage to hold him?" Andrus asked. "None of us could ever pin that guy when we sparred.

I shrugged. "Rage?"

They found that answer as good as any. After a while, Hadi rejoined us, a melancholy grin on his face.

"We can come back here, you know?" I said. "I plan on going on lots of time tours when this is over."

The dragon sighed. "That would be wonderful. I will miss this place."

"Do you need to make arrangements with the other priests?" I asked.

He waved his hand. "Them, I will not miss. They'll replace me without a second thought. I am the pharaoh's favorite, so the rest of the priests hold a grudge."

"You can't help but make friends wherever you go," said Felix.

Hadi grinned. "Jealous?"

Felix flipped him off.

"Alright," I said. "Let's get going."

The fires in the courtyard and the smaller one in the temple itself guttered out. "No. Just no, to whatever's happening," I said.

"Gareth." The voice that spoke his name was smooth, and rich, and sultry.

"Damn," he whispered, shooting me an apologetic look.

The darkness peeled back to reveal a tall, slender woman with feathers along the underside of her arms. Every step she took, her hips undulated in a hypnotizing display.

"I think you've been avoiding me, wolf," said the goddess. Her white robe was a gauzy, see-through material, billowing in a breeze that hadn't been there a moment earlier. Red stain glistened on her lips, and the black charcoal around her eyes made her bright green irises glow all the brighter.

Her straight black hair hung down her back in a river of obsidian and she was crowned with a simple gold circlet. She only had eyes for Gareth, her luminous smile unable to hide the raw desire smoldering within her.

Right behind her, peering from the darkness, was Ammit, devourer of souls unworthy of the afterlife.

"Maat," said Gareth, bowing his head. "*Avoiding* is a strong word. I'm not worthy of the kind of attentions you lavish me with."

She laughed, a dark, sultry sound as her eyes flashed. "You know I can tell a lie when I hear one."

"Yes," he acknowledged. "Then you'll also know it's not a lie when I say I'm mated to this woman. The Titans' daughter."

Maat's face soured to a pucker. "The construct that's supposed to set them free?"

I nodded. "Nice to meet you." Suck on that lie.

"It doesn't matter," she said, turning back to Gareth. "I'll give you one last chance to see reason." She stepped up to him and placed her hands on his chest. The wolf was uncomfortable beyond anything else he'd dealt with in the last few days.

"You and I will be great together. You are a valiant man. We're made for each other," she said.

Gareth took her hands and pushed them away firmly. "No, Maat. I'm sorry, but my heart belongs to another."

Andrus made a disbelieving noise, and Hadi took a step toward me at the same time my stomach bottomed out. He shouldn't have said that. Why did he say that?

Maat's face twisted. "Fine. If that's how you want to play it." Her sultry smile was replaced by a scowl as she snapped her fingers.

The world dissolved and when it reappeared, we were in a throne room. The throne itself stood empty, but the giant set of scales set in the middle of the room, copper gone green with patina, said enough about where we were.

"Are you ready to be weighed, measured, and found wanting?" Maat asked, grabbing me around the arm. When my mates tried to intervene, a single wave of the hand was all it took to freeze them in place. Their eyes still moved as they watched my progress toward the scales.

"Let's see what the scales have to say."

Ammit moved into full view now, his greenish-gray body covered in thick, greasy hair and his elongated jaws slavering in anticipation of a meal.

What do I do? I sought frantically for any idea, but nothing came. Maat formed her hand into a claw and plunged it into my chest, wrenching my heart free before I could even scream. I stared at it as it beat in her hand, like something out of *Indiana Jones*.

Her bare feet smacked on the stone floor as she moved to the scales, setting my heart on one side and plucking a feather from her arm to set on the other.

"I'm not sure how fair this is," I said. "There should be different rules for constructs."

The scales wavered back and forth, the creak of the mechanisms the only sound. Not being able to sense my heartbeat but otherwise feeling no ill effects of having my heart ripped out was a hell of an existential experience.

Maat said nothing, so I tried again. "The Fates are the ones in control here. You don't have a say. And I don't think they'll appreciate you stepping on their toes."

She scoffed. "The Fates? A long-faded fairy story of no consequence."

"How can you of all people say that?" I asked. "You don't believe in fate?"

"I don't believe in *the* Fates," she clarified. "They haven't been seen or heard from in ages. They don't care for this world anymore."

"Then why don't we take it up with them directly?" I asked. I was bluffing, but I hoped she wouldn't call it. I had no idea how to find them, or if we could even approach them.

The goddess regarded me, tapping a finger against her chin. "You know what? Let's. I think you'll be surprised at how little they have to do with anything. This can be an eye-opener for you."

She said it in a way that implied she knew exactly what she was walking into. She snapped her fingers again and it was just the two of us and Ammit. I couldn't see two feet in front of me and realized we were in a cave.

Maat lit a ball of witch fire to guide us. The tunnels had no rhyme or reason, but Maat seemed to know where she was going. The lumbering form of Ammit trailed behind. It gave me the creeps to have that beast following me in the dark, but I'd just have to have faith that it wouldn't try to take a bite out of me.

She stopped and I realized there was a wall in front of us about an inch before I ran into it.

"We seem to have hit a dead end," I said, stating the obvious just to fill the silence.

"Are you ready?" she asked.

No.

"Okay," I said, backing up as she placed her hand on the wall. A design etched into the stone glowed and then the entire section sank back and disappeared.

It was a continuation of the pitch black as I stepped through and Maat followed with her light, letting it float up toward the ceiling. A squeaking noise was the only sign of life, like an old door with rusty hinges. She fed more power to the light overhead and the room came into focus.

"What is this?" I asked.

Spiderwebs hung thick on everything, glittering in the light. The noise got louder as I made my way forward. My foot kicked something wooden, and it skittered off across the floor, landing at the feet of—

My heart leaped to my throat. A shrouded figure sat in a rickety chair in front of a wooden spinning wheel, long stilled and covered in cobwebs.

The figure wasn't moving. Another figure stood behind the wheel and another kneeled beside it. I peered into the shrouds.

"Gods," I breathed, bile rising in my throat. I was staring at mummified faces and then I noticed the spinning wheel again. On the spindle, stabbed clean through, was a desiccated eyeball, plucked out from the root.

"What happened here?" I asked.

Maat chuckled. "It's obvious isn't it? Your Fates are dead."

Coming Soon

The Death's Left Hand Series:
Coiled Phantoms: Kairos (Book 4) – November 12th, 2024

The Primordial Embers Series Concludes...
Look for a new release EVERY MONTH, six novellas in total!
Look for Book 6 in the series November 27th, 2024

Visit gwydionroyce.com or follow @gwydionroyce on insta-
gram and facebook for the latest updates!

The Catalog

The Death's Left Hand Series:
(Dark Paranormal Urban Fantasy)
Book 1: Iron-Forge Crossroads: Metanoia
Book 2: Iron-Forge Crossroads: Remeant
Book 3: Coiled Phantoms: Exuvia

The Primordial Embers Series:
(Reverse Harem Dark Fantasy Romance)
Book 1: Trickster's Ashes
Book 2: Illusion Razed
Book 3: Stone Captive
Book 4 : Enemies Remade
Book 5: Primordial Fall